EXORCISING THE GOODIE

By

Jane Mudrovich

[signature: Jane Mudrovich]

Strategic Book Publishing and Rights Co.

Book Design/Layout by Kalpart. Visit www.kalpart.com

Strategic Book Publishing and Rights Co.
12620 FM 1960, Suite A4-507
Houston TX 77065
www.sbpra.com

ISBN: 978-1-61897-939-1

DEDICATION

To Violet Jane
who was always smarter than me.

ACKNOWLEDGEMENTS

I would like to extend my appreciation to Tom for accepting THE GOOGIE and finding its worth, to Kermit, Jennifer and Matthew for their support and encouragement, to Larry for his insistence that I finish Lilly's story, to Michael for his early reading and friendship, and to my family of origin for its wealth of life.
Lastly, I would like to thank Mr. King for keeping me constantly interested enough to read his stories and nurturing in me an avid fan of the printed word.

CONTENTS

Chapter 1.

THE WAKE

Baba's house was loaded with relatives the week she lay dying in a coma. It was a seven-day reunion of locals and out-of-towners. I had never seen some of these people before as they had married or were born into families living in faraway places. Others had accents and wore strange clothes. Cousins from California said bitchin', and tits and cherry often and with ease as if bitchin' and tits were part of everyone's daily vocabulary. When I tried these words out for myself, I felt stupid, but this was not the case for Violet Jane who got right into the swing of things, speaking her new found Beach Boy lingo like a seasoned surfer. I knew when we went back to school these cool bits of foreign slang would be strategically rationed on her adoring toadies. Violet would be very bitchin' and they would be very cherry regardless of who had any tits.

Married cousins with babies came in from Detroit. The men brought their own beer and kept a keen eye on their glittery wristwatches. Card tables were set up in Baba's living room, and while the men played card games under clouds of cigarette smoke and piles of money, their women gossiped in the kitchen over kettles of Serbo-Croatian foods. The women gossiped in the kitchen, putting together a veritable feast of roast leg of lamb, cabbage rolls and ham hocks in sauerkraut, chicken and dumplings in paprika, parsley potatoes, tomato and cucumber salad, honey nut breads, and cheese and apple strudels.

No one arrived at my grandma's house without a platter of pastries, a pocketful of jokes and a wad of wet handkerchiefs. Evenings were spent at the dining room table over-eating and over-drinking as aunts and uncles toasted each other and Baba with liberal shots of slivovitz, whiskey and water. We rabble of cousins listened transfixed at our parents' elbows, nursing our own bottles of colored pop, while the adults spun childhood yarns of mystics and misdemeanors. Some of us snuck liquor from our parents' unattended highballs, while others lifted whole unopened bottles of beer from the Detroit gang. Violet Jane rehearsed her new California slang out behind the barn and coughed through a dozen Lucky Strikes.

The boy cousins thought she was really bitchin, especially Wilson, whose father was a used car salesman. No one seemed to care that Wilson and Violet sat in his dad's car, smoking cigarettes and listening to the radio, wearing down the battery. Sometimes Cousin Boo and I slouched in the back seat, jackstrawed across its upholstered couch.

No one noticed when Wilson took us for a drive around the neighborhood. Driving since he was six-and-a-half years old, I guess everyone figured Wilson knew what he was doing, and at twelve, he no longer had to stand up to reach the pedals.

After Baba's funeral, and after the California and Detroit relatives left, life reverted to more than to its usual echo. Party over, their leaving created an even greater vacuum with each parting family, as if life had only existed during the week they had lived in my grandmother's house. More alone now with her and them gone, I grew more and more lost without the continued sustenance of the out-of-towners whose families seemed more real than my own.

Dad said that when people die, it's like falling off a cliff. He did a hand dive bomb.

"That's it. Done. Turn into dirt in the end."

He said he did not believe in life after death. He said, "If thirteen years of Catholic school crammed down my throat won't get me into heaven, then to hell with it."

I lived most of my life behind the TV screen, actively participating in families that regularly showed up every weekday and weekend. I wished The Beaver was my brother and Wally was my boyfriend--- you could keep Eddie Haskell. Ricky Nelson was the coolest. During the week, I waited around after school for Spin and Marty to come in from the ranch. Miss Kitty was my Saturday night idol while Dad liked Marshall Matt Dillon, even though his boots looked like they dragged on the ground either side of his horse. When I was a kid, Soupy Sales used to knock me out, eyeballing the camera and screwing around with that crazy bow tie. "Luh oh oh," said Blacktooth and White Fang. Television people had fun. Brothers and sisters got along nicely. Involved parents and their well-dressed kids figured things out together. They communicated. In one half-hour, families went from tragedies to smiles and hugs and pats on the back. In my house, Mom was too busy, Dad was too tired, Hyacinth was never home, Violet couldn't stand me, and Baba was hurtling off the cliff and turning into dirt.

Chapter 2.

THE PROM

Charlie Freeber was a big sweaty boy with a head like a bucket. Nothing about him was tits or cherry since he wasn't a dreamboat and since Violet Jane's bitchin' California slang got constipated about two weeks into sixth grade. Freeber played the tuba in the band at Decantor Junior High School in Custer, Michigan where I spent eighth grade. I ended up going to the junior prom with him.

"Violet tells me Charles Freeber has asked you to the prom," Mom said, stirring the frothing pot of canned peas as she caught me stealing past the kitchen doorway. She's been in the kitchen working at supper like it's a race, and she's trying to set a new world record. Every move's a short cut to the finish line with a pot and pan on every burner, heat cranked up to HI on all of them, empty tin cans strewn across the countertop and cupboard doors slamming in rhythm; she's holding her own.

"Huh?" I hunched up in my tracks.

"Well?" she turned, wiping her hands on the lap of her apron. She shimmied something brown in a skillet

Darn that Violet!

"I hope you know that you're going." She threw me a one-eyed shot.

"Mommmmm."

"Don't mom me. You're going," she insisted, closing the refrigerator door with her hip. Then, as is if this was the real selling point: "You'll be seen."

"Seen?! That's the bad part." I slouched in the doorway, steering out of her line of fire.

"Isn't he Max Freeber's boy?" she asked over a splattering pot.

"How should I know?"

"Sure, Max and Shirley Freeber," Mom nodded to herself. "I never did like him, but Shirley's in the PTA. They're a nice family. Ouch!"

She tossed the lid off a volcanic brew of green lava flowing over the pot, scorching into the already blackened ash under the burner.

"What's that got to do with Freeber? " I protested.

"You're going and that's that," she said, licking her finger.

"Just because someone asks me doesn't mean I have to go."

"Did anyone else ask you?" Mom gave me one of her looks, momentarily taking her eyes off the stove and risking another catastrophe.

"No," I said, checking out something on my shoe.

"Now, when is this little affair?" she asked, shaking paprika into a roiling pot.

"Next week."

Hammering a wooden spoon on the rim of a pan, she asked, "when next week?"

"Saturday." I can see the gallows swinging in the breeze, the writing on the wall. I can see Violet Jane and her cronies reconnoitering like hyenas in some dark corner of the gymnasium, plotting their ambush as the Beach Boys carry on about a girl named Rhonda helping them do something to get someone else out of their hair, and out of breath, sweaty Charlie Freeber steering me around the basketball floor backward into the herd. This will give my twin sister Violet Jane a lot of ammo for future use. I'm just about getting tears in my eyes thinking about it.

"Doesn't give us much time to find you a nice gown," Mom broke into my happy thoughts. "What? Lilly! Don't start with that face. You should be happy to go to the prom with Charles Freeber. Why, when I was your age I'd have given my eyeteeth to go to a prom. Any prom. You wouldn't believe what I endured growing up. You're thin now, but when I was a young girl thin was not fashionable. I was so undernourished they thought I had TB. I lost my sense of smell. The health department came to the house to talk to Baba and Jeda, and don't you think that was fun?"

She's on a roll clanking spoons on pots and pans.

"You had to have some meat on your bones. As poor as we were and foreigners living in the East End? Why it was hard enough just to go to school."

Some poor pan got an extra hard bonk on its rim.

Pretty soon I knew I was going to hear about the onion fields.

"You don't realize how lucky you are," she pushed. "I worked my fingers to the bone picking onions to buy myself a pair of shoes!"

"How lucky is it to go to the biggest school dance with a guy who sweats all the time? He's always breathing hard and his face is always red and he wears a suit to school."

I slumped against the counter. "Kids don't wear suits to school Mom. He's such a dork."

"Lucky."

And that's that.

"Now get in here and set the table. Call your father and your sisters for dinner. It's time to eat. We'll talk about your gown later and I'm sure Violet will need one, too."

I could almost see the light bulb go on.

"Maybe you two can sew them yourselves. We'll go down to Klein's Department Store and pick out a pattern and material this weekend."

The noose tightened.

Like a card dealer, Mom clattered bowls, platters, and serving spoons onto the counter top, pouring and scraping brown, green, and beige clumps of various sizes into their containers. Spoons clattered into bowls. Time! A new world record was set. Surveying the wreckage of pots and pans sitting crazy-stacked on the stove and in the sink, caked and scorched, hard-drying as fast as they could, I suddenly remembered it was my turn to wash the dishes.

***

Locking a bathroom door in our house was a crime, but I did it anyway. I drew the window shade against old man Kreps' place next door. (Violet claimed he grabbed her butt once when Mom sent her over with a plate of oatmeal cookies. He's only about a hundred-and-fifty years old, but I guess he got around pretty good when he had a reason.) I stood in front of the medicine chest mirror, trying out new strategies to improve my figure. Maybe if I stood up really, really straight, chest out, stomach in, something magical would happen. Maybe something girl-like would show up. I looked okay from the front. Not too bad. Let's try the side view. I looked like I was six.

Knock. Knock. Knock.

"What are you doing in there?"

It was Violet. "Nothing."

"Mom!" she called down the stairs, "Lilly's in the bathroom with the door locked!"

I could see her squinting into the keyhole.

"Looking at yourself, huh? You think you're suddenly going to sprout boobs in a week? You're so stupid."

She wrenched the doorknob back and forth.

"Ma!"

"What is it now?"

I heard Mom through the floor from the vicinity of the TV room.

"Will you two stop arguing and start cleaning up the kitchen?!"

She called, "Lilly, you know you girls are not supposed to lock that door!"

I thought I heard her say something to Dad.

"Ha. Ha. Ha."

Sounding self-satisfied Violet got back to the matter at hand.

"What are you going to do about the rest of you? Like your flat chest is the *only* thing you got to worry about."

My twin had no chest either, but she had belted in her waist so she could squeeze out twenty-one inches, giving herself a couple of curves.

She thought she was Scarlett O'Hara.

"At least I'm going to the prom with a *guy*," I muttered, skulking out of the bathroom past Violet who, quick as a cat, stuck out one of her big clunky saddle shoes, tripping me.

Fighting to right myself, I stomped about so as not to take a header down the stairway. Far away a newspaper rattled. Dad's La-Z-Boy recliner collapsed, and heavy footsteps followed.

Down at the bottom of the stairway, Dad waited, holding The Custer Evening News between the fingers of one large hand. (Big Pete, his buddies called him; Dad stood six-feet-five-inches tall and weighed in at 280 pounds. He had wavy black hair and clear blue eyes and generally lived in white t-shirts and blue jeans. I could smell his Old Spice before I saw him.)

"I thought your mother told you two to stop monkeying around."

He's the only person I ever knew who actually said monkeying around. It was very cherry.

Dad and I looked at each other. Violet Jane was nowhere to be found.

"Where's your sister?" he asked.

I shrugged my shoulders.

"Didn't your mother tell you two to get started on the dishes?"

"Uh huh."

I plodded down the stairway.

***

Mother says I was a sullen child. She says I was lazy. I don't think I was sullen or lazy. What happened was I got lost sometimes. Not sure where I went in my brain, but I went someplace because I'd remember coming back. I got lost pretty much everywhere I went: home, church (especially), and school. It was easy to hang out in my head at Decanter Junior High School because of its tall classroom windows where I regularly watched dogs, cats, cars, birds, bugs, trees, grass, and clouds, while still sitting in my chair. Daydreaming was where I lived--except for art class. I was pretty good in art since I was a kid. I drew and colored all the time. Once when I was five years old and drew a particularly good picture of a house with trees and flowers around it, I walked in on Mom and Dad in the bathroom.

I thought it was just Mom, since we all walked in on her when she was in there. She said it was like Grand Central Station when she was in the bathroom. This particular time, however, it was Dad who rushed to the door. He covered his private parts with one hand and turned me around with the other hand saying "yah, yah, yah, very nice," and locked the door behind me.

***

Hyacinth Suzanne, my oldest sister, usually cooked supper when Dad worked the afternoon shift at Consolidated Paper Products. Violet and I mopped and waxed the kitchen and bathroom floors every Saturday regardless. We scrubbed toilets and washed windows. We took turns pushing the Hoover vacuum cleaner around the house, and we Pledged everything. We got drafted into the dishes brigade. One week I'd wash the dishes and Violet would dry; the next week she'd wash, and I'd dry. The drying person also hauled the garbage out to the curb at the end of the driveway---usually in the dark. Once during a late night curb drop, Violet locked herself out of the house and *swears* The Giggler (mentally deranged maniac once rumored to be on the loose in our neighborhood, possibly a victim from a radiation accident at the Lake Erie Nuclear Power Plant) was breathing down her neck at the back door. She claims she actually *heard* him when she broke off the door handle. I didn't hear anything as I was seriously into my bowl of Neapolitan ice cream with nut sprinkles and Hershey's chocolate syrup poured over the top. Twilight Zone was on in the TV room, and I was nicely curled in Dad's recliner. Violet ended up ringing the front door bell which I *did* hear, but not before Mom and Dad did too, and they were already in bed.

***

The eighth grade Decanter Junior High School Prom was an adventure, I guess you'd say. Mom got the whole thing started with pictures of what she called "the handsome couple." Freeber and I posed together and separately on the porch in front of the picture window where Violet Jane crouched inside the house making puking sounds which nobody acted like they heard. Since Freeber managed the invite, he was responsible for the transportation. His mother, Shirley, who Mom liked because of the PTA thing, thought we were a "darling couple." They chatted like old friends about how fast their

15

children had grown up and how they remembered it was only yesterday they were taking us to our first day of kindergarten. Charlie Freeber looked about as embarrassed as me, sweating in his "monkey suit" (another of Dad's terms, this one for any type of men's formal dressing apparel). My gown, in the most general sense of the word, and sewn by yours truly, was made of taffeta with small blue roses on a white background replete with sash and ruffled half-slip to give it that frilly feminine touch. Freeber stuck me with a hatpin several times before Mom stepped in to secure the ribbon and orchid corsage, the bodice of my prom dress sagging due to the weight of too much corsage and not enough boobs. It was 7:45 PM.

The official Decanter Junior High School Prom didn't start until eight o'clock, but Freeber wanted to get there early so we could get a good seat in the bleachers. The bottom row was best because it left an easy access to the dance floor, food, and bathrooms. The popular kids staked claim to the top tier sucking face and playing hide and seek in each other's underwear. It was dark up there in the rafters but chaperones didn't see too well that far away; plus, they would have had to crawl through the crowd in their high heels and party clothes.

"Hey Lilly, what's A squared plus B squared?" Violet called out as we--the handsome couple--passed by the punch bowl on our way to the cookies.

"What'd she say?" Freeber asked.

"Nothing," I said.

"I said what's A squared plus B squared equal?" Violet cheerily volunteered a little louder.

She already had some of her toadies with her.

"A squared plus B squared. Isn't that algebra?" Freeber wondered out loud.

"Yeah, that's algebra all right," Violet chirped, behind her chipped front tooth.

She flipped me the bird and slunk away into the prom traffic.

"What'd she mean by that?" Freeber asked again.

"I don't know."

Of course, I knew what she meant; as Violet Jane wanted to

remind me of the incident last fall when I took a header in front of the bleachers. I'd been happily pretend-skating around the gymnasium floor in my black and white saddle shoes. I had on this cute little green and blue plaid skirt, minding my own business, mapping out circles and shapes on the gymnasium tiles, and doing a little geometry in my head. It was one of those lost times, you see. I'd wolfed down my green Jell-O, macaroni and cheese, slice of white bread with a pat of yellow margarine on the side, and a carton of white milk so I could get in a couple of dances before going back to class. The Beatles were begging to hold my hand over the loud speakers: Life was pretty good. *This is a semi-circle,* I thought to myself. *This is a rectangle which I can find the diagonal to if I know the length and width,* when a particularly large wad of juicy fruit gum grabbed my shoe. Originally I'd been hidden in the throng of other dancers and stand-a rounds, but when I bopped a few classmates on their heads and chests, they gave me a wide berth. Perhaps they thought I'd learned a new dance step. I flailed about ever so briefly before sprawling backward, knees up and out, about three feet from the boys in the bleachers. Later, thanks to Debbie Barstow, I saw just how spectacular I'd been, shucked out on the gymnasium floor, as she reenacted the event for me on Margie Lathrup's front lawn while walking home from school. She laughed so hard she wet herself. It wasn't until I was safely ensconced in the upstairs bathroom of my own house that I reenacted the scene to discover two dime-sized holes right in the middle of my cotton underpants. Freeber was still eating in the cafeteria that fateful day and missed my big audition.

The evening progressed. The punch was sweet. The cookies were chocolaty. The potato chips were ruffled, and the French onion dip was all ours. Since neither Freeber nor I cared about our breath we hung around the chips and dips and those little barbeque wieners on a toothpick.

Losing myself in the music, I closed my eyes into the sway of the dance. My head laid on his shoulder as we moved with the rhythm of the others under the crepe-paper canopy. It was sort of romantic. I started to think Charlie Freeber wasn't so bad. His head was sort of big and everything, and he sweated up a storm, but the Old Spice he wore was nice, like Dad's.

"So did you know I was going to ask you to the prom?"

We'd just finished a couple of go-rounds and stopped back at the food table. Romance over. Charlie was red-faced and breathing hard. His suit had lost its starch. The side of my face was damp and so was the front of my dress; the orchids hung sideways down my bodice.

"Yeah."

"How did you know?" he asked.

"Violet told me."

"How'd she know?"

"I guess Billie Sue Bedner heard it from Nancy Turkel who heard it from Bobby Johnson who sits next to you in band."

I pulled my wilted dress away from my chest.

"Oh."

Charlie hit the chips and dips, hard. He grabbed a napkin and mopped his forehead.

"You want some punch?"

"I guess."

"So how's it going, Spider?" Frankie Banyon steered Shelly Fritz out of the twirling crowd of happy promsters.

Frankie and I had fifth hour art class together with Mr. Baumgartner. We sat at the same table. Frankie hated it when I got a better grade than he did. He never called me by my given name.

"Okay," I said.

"I see you're here with ole Freeber," he smirked. "I heard he was going to ask you."

"Spider? Why does Frankie call you Spider?" Shelly wanted to know.

"Look at her," Frankie put out his arm and levered it up and down.

"Long legs. You know, Daddy Long legs," he chuckled. "Spider."

Shelly chuckled, too.

Charlie returned with two plastic cups of fruit punch.

"Hey, how's it going, Banyon?"

He handed a cup to me.

"It's alright," Frankie said.

Shelly chuckled again. I decided Shelly Fritz was an idiot. "I need to go to the little girls' room," Shelly said, coyly.

Frankie smiled at us.

"Women," he said, "can't live with them. Can't live without them. See you around, Spider."

We watched them spin into the madding crowd.

"I think your legs are sexy," Charlie said.

Cherry Fruit Punch sucked down the wrong pipe. I coughed and hacked, doubled over and stomped on the floor with my white party pumps. Charlie slapped me a few good whacks on the back and asked if I needed anything.

"Wrong pipe," I croaked.

"Jump up and down."

He leaned over.

"My mother always tells us kids to jump up and down when we get something stuck in our throats."

He stood up, paused in thought.

"Although one time, she picked up my little sister by her feet and turned her upside down and gave her a couple of good shakes. It worked."

He looked at me.

"You might be too big for that, but I could try if you wanted."

What? I tried to hit myself on the back.

Charlie administered two swift raps. I ralphed up enough pink party punch into a napkin to breathe through my mouth, snorted a good-sized gob, coughed again, got another whack from Charlie for good measure, and felt much better.

"You want a drink of water?" he asked.

"Bathroom," I gasped, and clomped away.

"You want me to come with you?" Charlie called.

I shook my head "no" and groped my way to the lady's room, smeared in sweat, cherry fruit punch flavored snot, and saliva. I held both my hands straight out in front of me like a blind person.

"I'll just wait right here," Charlie said.

I waved at him behind my back.

"Christ, Lilly, you look like crap."

It was Violet. She was in the bathroom cinching in her waist, trying for another half inch. Cigarette smoke hung over her bobbed hairdo like a cloud. Two members of her fan club were sitting in the stalls with the doors open. Barbara had her prom dress hiked up and her party shoes off. Bonnie Sue was balling up another stick of Juicy Fruit gum in her mouth.

"Geez," I wheezed, and coughed, stomped again.

"You're a mess."

Satisfied with her waist for the moment, Violet bent into the mirror threatening an ornery curl on her cheek.

"Went down the wrong pipe."

I leaned over the sink and turned on the cold water faucet.

"Que pasa nina? You look *muy crapolita."*

Violet's favorite word was crap in any of its conjugations. She had an arsenal of favorite suffixes generally disregarding language rules of grammar or national origin. Second hour Spanish class with Senior Madria had given my twin sister a veritable cornucopia of new combinations to try out. Violet wore her bilingual talents with pride.

I wiped pink mucus from my face. Bonnie Sue snapped her gum and Barbara rustled her dress. "Yeah, what'd you do? Puke on yourself?" one of them said.

I stood up, taking a deeper breath.

"Punch went down the wrong pipe."

"Bend back down over the sink," Violet ordered.

I obliged. I always obliged Violet Jane. She was cool, and I was lost in space. On the rare occasion when she let me in on her latest social acquisition, it was under duress and without explanation as to meaning. Usually, I was left to stumble through life by myself, hamstrung in my own distracted thoughts. (Violet also collected invaluable news items on celebrities and the odd and the strange as if they were homework assignments. *TV Guide* and *The National*

Enquirer were two of her cherished periodicals.)

A cool paper towel was laid across the back of my neck.

"Here, this will relax you," Violet spoke to me quietly.

"Hey, Charlie Freeber wants to know if Lilly's all right," Connie Jenkins burst through the bathroom door.

"What happened?"

Violet balled up the damp paper towel she'd placed on my neck and tossed it into the garbage can.

"Lilly barfed on that crappy rot-gut Kool-Aid."

I straightened up. "Went down the wrong pipe. Phew. Think I'm okay now."

"Let's get out of here," Violet spoke to her troupes.

"Supposed to be a lady's choice coming up pretty quick, and I don't want to miss it because I'm stuck in this damn shithouse screwing around with you guys."

Violet checked herself out in the mirror.

"I think that David Schuster is *muy simpatico.*"

Gum snapped in succession, party shoes clomped under foot, dresses rustled.

"*Adios moy sestra*

Violet sashayed like royalty with her toadies in tow.

"Your girlfriend will be out *en uno minuto*," I heard her tell Freeber.

***

I waited on the curb for Freeber to open the door. Mom warned me to wait for the gentleman to open the door. Young ladies wait, she said. The cooling air was both refreshing and soothing. After the heat of the gymnasium and the befouling I'd done to myself, I didn't feel so good. Max Freeber had waited for us in his highly polished Buick Electra convertible, fire-engine red, white-walled tires, white leather interior. Even I, who knew nothing about cars and felt decidedly unwell, thought this ride was very cool. It was big as a tank with a back seat like a couch.

"You two kids have fun?" he asked around a fat cigar. (I could see the resemblance from father to son, as Mr. Freeber's head was a big round block too. And sweaty. The resemblance was remarkable.

21

I looked in the side view mirror and wondered about the size of my own head. Seemed too small all of a sudden.)

Charles said yeah about having fun and walked around to the other side of the car. He opened the door and scooted over into the middle of the backseat, leaving me hemmed in.

"You want the windows up?" Mr. Freeber adjusted his rearview mirror.

"I'm okay," I answered.

"You need to be right home?" he asked. Cigar smoke in. Cigar smoke out.

"I don't know. I guess."

Boy, was his head big. These were some large headed people. I wondered what their heads weighed. Bet it was over seven pounds. Maybe fourteen. I wondered what Freeber's mom's head looked like. The land of the giant potato heads. Mr. and Mrs. Potatohead and son, Spud. Ha. Ha. Spud. I wondered what Violet would say.

"What about a little spin around the old block? Just got this baby all dressed up and no place to go." Max Freeber caressed his baby's smooth padded dash. "Feel like a ride? She handles real smooth. What'd you say, Chuckie? Feel like taking your girl out for a little spin?"

Your girl? Not me, I'm not. Yikes!

"If it doesn't take too long." Chuckie looked at me. "I think Lilly's parents are expecting her home."

I was still stuck on the your girl part. And Chuckie? Geez.

"Won't take long." Mr. Freeber puffed. "You've got to live a little.. How often do you get to ride around in a beauty like this baby? Huh?"

He rolled his cigar around in his mouth, took a drag, puffed out a cloud.

"How about some music?"

Green dials came to life on the control panel. Old '50s rock and roll rang out about smoke getting in my eyes, which I thought was pretty coincidental.

"Cool car," I admitted, glad the top was rolled back since I got carsick easily. Music was kind of nice. Old and familiar. Night air felt good. I guessed a short little jaunt around the neighborhood in this fancy-dancy red super-duper automobile was okay. I mean, how long did it take anyway? Ten minutes? I felt pretty cool myself now that I thought of it. Yeah, I was ready for a little spin around the block. Sure, why not? Can't hurt. Just me and the two talking heads.

The little spin turned out to be a carnival ride through downtown Custer. My neatly coiffed party 'do flew up from behind my unprotected, tiny skull, scratching my cheeks and eyeballs and catching in my teeth. Starched lace petticoats billowed up, snagging on the hatpin holding my corsage, exposing silk stockings, garter belt and thigh. Chuckie said something, but I didn't know what. I didn't get it the second time either. We wrestled taffeta and under netting from the wilted flowers dragging down the front of my gown, scooping handfuls of dress and slip around my legs. We careened around corners in the big red tank of a car. We raced from traffic light to traffic light. Max Freeber sang along with the radio, clearly enjoying himself, oblivious to his wards in the back seat. While joyriding, he pitched me against his son or slammed me against the door to which I clung dearly. When I shivered in the wind, Charlie put a heavy arm around my shoulders, warming me and scaring me at the same time. His suit coat was damp. His sweat seeped into my dress, sticking taffeta to me and me to him. Memories of Old Spice cologne wafted up between us.

Once, when we stopped for a traffic light, Charlie asked if I wanted to go out with him. Practically brain dead from the ride from hell, I told him I thought we already were out. No, he said. he meant to go out steady as in boyfriend girlfriend. I think Mr. Freeber heard us as I saw a corner of his mouth curl up.

Oh my God.

"I'm not old enough to date," I said, which was the truth. But, geez, I've got to get out of here. Where were we anyway? I pulled myself up to the back of the front seat.

"Mr. Freeber?" I asked. "How far are we from my house?"

"What? Had enough already?" he laughed. Cigar smoke in. Cigar smoke out.

"But if you were?" Charlie persisted.

"I think I'd better get home." Trapped like a rat, I was; plus, the cigar smoke was starting to make me a teeny bit nauseous.

When we motored up the driveway to my house, I nearly wept. Miss Manners be damned, I unlocked and opened my side of the car door before Mr. Freeber had come to a complete stop. In my haste, I firmly stepped out onto the cement drive in my pretty white party shoe as Max Freeber's big red tank of a car quietly rolled over the back of my foot.

"Thanks for the ride," I managed, as I hobbled from the vehicle. "Bye."

Charlie scrambled after me from his side of the car unaware of my mishap.

When I grabbed the backdoor handle, I found it locked. Knock. Knock. Knock. Charlie was closing in on me. I was stuck like a deer in the headlights. Knock. Knock. Knock. Violet's head peeked at me from the other side of the storm door.

"Violet Jane," I pleaded, standing on one foot. "Open the door!"

She giggled.

Knock. Knock. Knock. "Violet!" I was desperate.

"So, I had a really great time tonight, Lilly." Charlie had me trapped between himself and the door, his big head blocking out the car lights.

"Yeah, thanks," I said. "Violet, would you please open this door?"

"So maybe I'll see you at school on Monday."

"Yeah, maybe." *Since your locker's only next to mine.*

"Okay then." He waited, sweating and panting.

I wrenched the handle back and forth. "Vi o let!"

Suddenly the door sprang open, and I fell inside.

"Shut the hell up, dumb head, you'll wake Mom and Dad! They just went to bed. So did jug-head Freeber kiss you?" Violet made sucking sounds.

"Thanks for locking me out." I grabbed hold of the railing.

"So where have you been all this time? The dance was over about a half hour ago," Violet admonished. "Hey, whose car was that?"

24

"We went for a ride in Charlie's dad's car."

"*Verdad? Muy bonito.*"

I hobbled up the back stairway into the light of the kitchen. I looked down at the back of my ruined white party pump and sucked air.

These had been my first pair of "high heeled" shoes. What would Mom say? As I peeled out of my shoe, accordioned skin stretched from my heel to the vinyl before tearing free, leaving a large raw wound on the outer side of my heel and purple and blue bruising on the inner side. Red blood pooled onto the linoleum. Dots floated in front of my eyes.

"I need to sit down," I said.

"What the hell happened? You stick your foot in a meat grinder?" Violet wanted to know. She put her hand out, said "hang on," and left to get a chair, but I was on the floor before she came back.

"Christ, Lilly!" she clattered the chair in front of me. "What are you doing?"

"I don't know." At that point I didn't know much of anything. "I might be sick."

"Don't you dare puke all over the place," Violet ordered. "Get a hold of yourself."

"What's going on down there?" Mom called from upstairs. "Is that Lilly June?"

"Yeah," both Violet and I looked at each other.

"It's late. You girls get to bed. We'll talk in the morning." A door closed.

"Can you walk on that thing?" my twin asked. "If you can, it's not broken."

"I guess so. I mean, I walked into the house."

Together Violet and I wrestled me up from the kitchen floor and into the den. I sat down in Dad's recliner and propped up my mangled limb. Violet ran a hand towel under cold water and wrapped it around my injured foot. She gave me an aspirin from the bathroom medicine cabinet and a glass of water from the kitchen sink. When she asked me if I wanted one of Dad's Valiums, I said no. Violet and I sat together for a time watching TV and visiting.

25

"Did you see Shelly Fritz's boobs hanging out of her dress?" Violet asked. "They looked like they were gonna pop any minute. Probably the only reason Frankie goes out with her is to get at them jugs."

"Yeah," I agreed looking down at my chest, "but wouldn't it be nice to have at least some of them?"

When I peeled the now hardened and pasted cherry fruit punch glop from the bodice of my dress, my sister just looked at me.

"I don't know. Wait until she gets older, they'll be down at her ankles."

Violet had a point.

"Hey, isn't Shock Theater on?" She got up to change the channel and turn down the volume. "Maybe something really pukey is on like some guy with his face rotting off where you can see his skull and empty eyeball sockets with worms coming out or maybe The Giggler's ready to stab someone to death." Violet paused. "Maybe not The Giggler."

She didn't holler at me. She didn't call me dumb or stupid. Once in a while my twin sister Violet was okay. And this was one of those whiles.

Chapter 3.

THE TWINS

"Two? What?" Grandpa Milkovich thundered. "Only animals and Italians have litters," he stormed.

Angry with his daughter and her husband when their twin girls, Violet Jane and Lilly June arrived into the world, Pete Dragich, the Croat, was not to be appeased.

"Animals and Italians," he cursed. "Harrumph!"

This protestation had been shouted out in his native Serbian tongue along with a rash of ethnic slurs about Catholics. And swear words that I cannot repeat in my head let alone out loud for fear of burning forever in the broiling lake of fire underneath the world. Do not pass go. Do not collect two hundred dollars. Just go straight to Hell!

Nobody was ready for twins. Not my grandfather, not my grandmother, not Dad, not Mom, not the doctor. I was the first to show my squished bald head after what my mother had called a "terrible dry delivery." Fourteen minutes later my sister's tiny rear-end shown at the gate. The doctor, Old Doc Ames, who should have retired a decade earlier along with her archaic obstetrical equipment, had not known that two babies had been quietly cohabitating in Teresa Dragich's womb. Because all concerned parties had expected a single baby of indeterminate gender, my surprised parents had selected only one baby name for a girl child and only one baby name for a boy. Consequently, since I was first out of the hatch, my name was ready and waiting to be typed onto my wrist band: Lilly June Dragich. But my sister, who'd been an unknown entity during the prior nine months of our communal fetal development, did not have a chosen name for her tiny white wrist band. Legend has it that she lived nameless for about a week. They called her Baby Dragich Two. My guess is that this brief unlabeled period of her life had lasting effects. My guess is this is why Violet Jane Dragich tormented me most of my life.

***

Theya Milkovich was my maternal grandmother. We called her Baba. She wore her long gray hair in dual braids wrapped around her head. No makeup. Her apron served as both belt and brazier. Baba fastened her thick cotton stockings with a rubber band rolled just below the knee. On her feet, she laced sensible black nun's shoes. Baba's wardrobe never changed.

Juro Milkovich was my maternal grandfather. We called him Jeda. He looked like Joseph Stalin. He smoked a pipe and played with his handlebar moustache when he thought about things. Baba smelled of lavender soap. Jeda smelled of stale tobacco. They slept in separate bedrooms since forever. Baba's room was light, airy and hand-crocheted white lace. Jeda's bedroom was small, dark and scary. A browned and aged print of St. John the Baptist hung on the wall above his single bed. A pipe rested at his ashtray. Jeda died when Violet and I were five years old. His room became a primary attraction in our lives as we cousins imagined Jeda's ghost still inhabited his bedroom. Periodically, we dared each other to walk into his quarters.

Summers after Grandpa Jeda passed away, when Cousin Boo (her real name was Grace) and her mom came to visit, were spent at Baba's house washing walls, shaking rugs and waxing floors. We polished woodwork and rearranged the furniture. We helped our mothers to empty cupboards and box up articles that had outlived their usefulness. Sometimes Violet, Boo, and I prowled the abandoned attic for clues to its dark treasures, already primed by *true* tales of ghosts and other

Transylvanic activity in the windowless loft proved to be a boon for our imaginations---especially since the scar on the attic door was rumored to be made by Baba when she threw a cleaver into it to keep the evil spirits from descending onto her sleeping children. We opened trunks and pawed through dried photographs. We retold stories we'd heard our parents tell at holiday, and funerals.

"Do you think Jeda's ghost is up here?" Cousin Boo asked.

"Maybe he's trapped, required to roam this earthly domain for all that God cursing he used to do. Maybe he needs our help so he can finally rest," Violet said.

"Heaven or hell?" she whispered, eyes bright.

"Aunt Beulah says she knows someone who talks to dead people," Boo added.

"That's bullshit," Violet said.

"Violet?" Boo said, "You swear too much. I don't know how she talks to dead people. I heard her telling Ma. I wasn't supposed to hear, but I did. They thought I was outside."

Cousin Boo thought a moment.

"Ma thinks Aunt Beulah's off her rocker, anyway." She picked up a particularly dusty photograph. and blew across it.

When the attic door slammed shut, we three conspirators raced each other down the stairway and out onto the second floor hallway, stopping short of the narrow room where our grandfather used to sleep.

Shoved into the doorway of the small stale room, I stood transfixed. I saw where our grandfather's slippers still lay on the floor by the bed, where his pipe grew old and cracked in the astray since his death. On the wall, wrapped in animal skins, and holding a crooked staff for all eternity, St. John the Baptist kept guard over Jeda's things, unchanged.

"Touch his pipe." Violet pushed her elbow in my back.

"Yeah," Boo collaborated, "Go on."

"Do it, scaredy-cat." Violet shoved me into Jeda's room, "Do it or I'll close the door and lock you in."

"You wouldn't do that, would you?" Boo asked Violet.

"What do you think?" she sneered.

It did not matter that our grandfather had been big-hearted under his wild exterior. It did not matter that he had grown to cherish his twin granddaughters after the angry embarrassment of discovering his middle daughter had married a Croat and reproduced a "litter." It did not matter that Jeda had regularly walked with Violet and me, our hands safe in each of his big paws, to the corner market to buy sugar corn candy and Black Jack stick gum---touching his things was taboo.

What if Jeda's ghost is watching? I thought, and hunched my shoulders against the watchful eye of St. John the Baptist.

"I'm going to lock you in if you don't get a move on it," Violet threatened, holding one hand on the doorknob. Cousin Boo peered out from behind her.

I took a breath. And on tiptoe skulked to the famous ashtray where Jeda's pipe had waited undisturbed for so many months, years. Teeth marks peppered the mouthpiece.

"Hurry up," Violet hissed.

Tentatively, I held my breath and poked the pipe's black stem with my index finger. Nothing happened. Phew.

"Pick it up," Violet dared.

Carefully, I curled my thumb and forefinger around its worn stem and lifted Grandpa's pipe several inches. I counted to three in my head and then replaced it. I looked to Violet, hoping she was satisfied.

"Now put it in your mouth."

My sister was insatiable.

Holding my breath, I picked up the pipe, shut my eyes against St. John the Baptist, and put the pipe's opening to my lips. I closed my mouth around it. Surprising myself, I reflexively drew in a lungful of stale but pleasant tasting tobacco, like dried cherries.

"Wow," Cousin Boo whispered from behind Violet.

"What are you girls up to?"

We three trespassers looked at each other.

"I hope you're not getting into anything up there," Aunt Sophie continued to call from downstairs. "Grace, you and the twins, come on down now and have something to eat. It's lunchtime."

"You better not tell anyone you were in Jeda's room, Lilly, or we'll all get into trouble," Violet promised.

"Okay," I answered, somehow less scared, remembering the tangy cherry taste from my grandfather's pipe.

"Boo?" Violet demanded.

"Me, either." Boo shook her head.

***

My sister and I were fraternal twins, which means we grew from two separate fertilized eggs. I was blonde, a bit taller and heavier than my sister who was brunette and wiry. My twin was pale pink skinned and more suited to cold winter colors. I was not. I tanned in the summer. Both of us had blue eyes though mine were grayer and sometimes changeable. For the most part, Mother discontinued dressing us alike after our first birthday. We did, however, occasionally don the identical twin girl thing evidenced by the photo albums I've wandered through. There was even a picture of Jeda pushing Violet and me across their backyard on Orchard Street in a baby-buggy. In another old black and white print, he and I were both pushing Violet. I looked to be struggling between Grandpa and the buggy, arms stretched overhead straining for the handles while he pushed. My little ruffled dress hiked up, showing fancy white baby pants.

I, of course, don't remember this. I was only a toddler. I don't remember much of Juro Milkovich except that he scared me when Mom shoved Violet and me into his sick room where St. John the Baptist stood guard looking like a wolf. We were only five years old. Mom said we needed to *see* Grandpa. She said he was going to the hospital and that we might not *see* him again. And she was right: we didn't.

Memories of my childhood were generally not happy ones. I have more feeling memories than movie type filmstrips. Violet's memories were like half hour situation comedies that she continuously edited so she and the family could look more like the ones on television. Violet knew what was going on in the world. She was informed about things. She had her thumb on it.

***

Mom and Dad were peripheral characters in my life. Violet Jane was the main attraction. If she thought my foot was not broken because I could walk on it, then it must not be broken. But it ached something awful, a kind of drooling pain that pounded up into my brain and back down again. Up and down, up and down, splashing over my stomach in a kind of seasickness. I swallowed another aspirin before crawling up the stairs on my hands and knees. When my sore foot bumped against the stairway wall, I broke out into instant sweat and clung to the banister, waiting for the dots in my eyes to go away. The steps before me looked to be at least a hundred of them,

31

vanishing precariously into the darkness above where I was to be imprisoned for the rest of my life. An injured captive at the mercy of my tormentors. *Climb!* they demanded. *Climb to the top! Move on!* they called after me and cracked a whip. Trsh! Weary and bedraggled, I forced myself to the top of the stairway where I was allowed a stolen moment of rest. My next Herculean task was to traverse the expanse of hallway in an attempt to reach the bathroom where the weak filter from the nightlight haloed around the doorway. Using the wall for balance and hopping on my good foot, I willed myself onward, not to be defeated, no longer caring about sweats or dots. I knew I could do it. Almost there. I could see the light.

The doorknob was cool in my hand. I used it like a cane and swung open into the bathroom. I sat longer on the toilet than I needed to, thankful just to be sitting somewhere. While washing my hands, I studied myself in the mirror, figured I looked like a train wreck, and decided, under the circumstances, I could get away with not brushing my teeth or my hair, which was a rat's nest from the joyride about a hundred years ago in Freeber's dad's big red wind machine. Violet had given me a bottle of peroxide, cotton balls, a tube of antiseptic cream and bandages. She told me to take care of myself since she thought it would be better if I doctored up my own foot than if she did. I didn't want to look at my messed up heel, but Violet said I had to, so I did. She said it was like falling off a horse and getting back on, that looking at the problem was better than imagining it since our minds usually came up with worse stuff than the actual fact. When I unwrapped my heel, the back of my foot looked like a peeled tomato.

It was hard to lie down without bed sheets pressing against my wound. Clanging noises in my head competed with the brass band in my foot. After a while. I passed out and dreamt about insidious pupa-larva shapes that had the ability to communicate and think like humans. They chittered across each other. twitching and scritching with purpose and planning, before springing back like twisted balloons. They were violet-black, blood-red, and green-gray. They rose up into enormous telepathic entities, evil and knowing in their silent amplified clanging and crashing, threatening without voice or form. When I woke up, my ears were plugged, and my pajamas were soaked. Shadows changed.

I turned on the bedside lamp. Bleached in the alien light, I worried about the night. Something malevolent watched me behind the corner of my numbed brain; some slobbering thing who knew my name. Afraid to get out of bed, afraid not to, I lay still, silently weeping, wiping my eyes on my sleeve and my nose on the bedcover. What to do? What to do? After a while I decided breathing was a good idea. Then breathing deeper and slower. Maybe a glass of water would help. Maybe another aspirin. Maybe one of those valiums would be good, but they were downstairs in the bathroom closet at the back of the house behind the TV room. Too far to go in the dark quiet. Too far to go by myself.

Cautiously, I sat up and swung my legs over the side of the bed. Was the boogeyman lurking underneath, hand outstretched, regardless of the light? Was he back in his cave? I looked down between my feet and saw nothing but floor. So far, so good. When I opened the bedroom door, cool air washed over my face. I realized I'd been holding my breath again. *Breathe, Lilly. Come on.* Through the hallway I saw closed doors and heard the stentorian snores of my parents. Usually an irritating racket, their nighttime sounds were now comforting. There were real people out there. There were my nighttime family sounds. With renewed courage, I marshaled my strength, stood on both my feet and did not get dots in my eyes or break out into a sweat.

A bathroom at 3 o'clock in the morning is a sometimes lonely, sometimes eerie place. Everyone else in the house was sound asleep, safely tucked into the rhythms of their happy dreams while I limped around in the void. Leaning on the sink and squinting against the uncovered light bulb, I shook an aspirin into my hand and ran the tap until the water was cold. Holding the tiny white pill on my tongue, I cupped water in both hands and swallowed. I swallowed another handful. And one more. When I looked in the mirror, I saw myself looking back at me: no writhing, twitching, giant maggot peering into the mirror from behind my shoulder. I moved in closer. I studied my eyes, nose, and teeth. I stuck my tongue out and examined my throat, that thing that hangs down way in the back by where my tonsils used to be. It looked okay. Satisfied, I assessed my chin and neck, turning first to the right, then to the left. I brought my hands up to my face and studied their reflection and wondered if they looked the same from this view as opposed to straight on. Hmm. Familiar. I looked at my eyes again. noticing the golden auras around the pupils this side of the gray-blue irises. I leaned in closer yet, pondering what lay behind the blackness at the center of my eyes. *Were pupils really black? Was black really a color? Mr. Baumgartner said that black is not a color, but rather, the absence of color, so what am I looking at? Am I seeing into the abyss? I wonder. People say the eyes are the windows of the soul. Fascinating. So is it the soul I'm looking at? My soul? Is that it? So what exactly is the soul, anyway? Soul. S. O. U. L. If I spell it S. O. L. E., then I'm talking about my feet. How about the fish? How is that spelled? Is it the same as the soles on my feet?* Things to think about.

I stepped back from my reflection and took in the whole picture. The whole me. I peeled my pajama top away from my chest and looked down my front. I guessed for now, that these eyes and body parts were mine and not those of an alien presence that had taken up residence in my form in the middle of the night, exchanging me for one of their pods like in that movie. Just my same old parts. Just my same old me. I brushed my hair carefully, undoing the tangles from the night, keeping an eye on myself in the mirror, making sure, watching for changes. I ran my toothbrush over my teeth without any paste, sucked in another handful of water and splashed my face. One final look. Yup, only me.

Back in my bedroom, I shrugged out of my pajamas and put on fresh cotton ones. I replaced the damp pillowcase with a new one and fluffed it up, and turned out the light. For a while, I lay on my back and stared into the darkness, the absence of color, and thought about things. But the brass band marching up my leg, banged open the door of my thoughts, reminding me of my ruined foot. What would Mom say? She'd probably holler, like that would be something new. Maybe she wouldn't notice, like that would be a miracle. Maybe it would all be okay when I woke up in the morning, like magic, like when Baba fixed my broken arm when I was six years old and fell off the bunk bed. I remember the ache got so bad that I carried my left arm around in my right hand as if the friction caused from air molecules was too much pressure. I felt like throwing up. There wasn't any way it did not hurt. I remember Baba putting her hands on me and making her wishes. Baba.

My eyes stung in their sockets. It seemed so long ago my

grandmother was here, cooking her special rice pudding that she learned to make in the "Old Country," keeping it warm on the stove while she watched the sidewalks for signs of Violet and me coming home from school. Sometimes she sat on the couch by the picture window crocheting or, if the weather was good, she might have rocked on the front porch swing holding her knuckled hands in her lap. Babushka covering her wrapped braids, constant apron, sensible nun's shoes, Baba was solid, patient, and kind. She was easy to talk to, easy to be around. Baba had time. Baba had love.

So did Dad, when we were little. He loved us so we knew it.

***

I used to think Violet liked me but just couldn't act like it for some reason. At least, I hoped she liked me, somewhere in her skinny heart. Her feelings against me were not always loud things that other people could see; usually they were secret things. Her anger could be quiet, like a whisper, as if just thinking about me could suck all the air out of a room, a thought creeping from her head into mine. She had been careful and vigilant in her meanness. She made sure.

When Violet and I were kids, we used to go fishing with Dad. It was a big adventure with lots of fanfare. We'd shoot for early in the morning so we'd be "up with the chickens," as Dad put it, getting that first worm. We traipsed around in the wet grass the night before, scouting for night crawlers that had screwed themselves out of the ground. Dad held the flashlight while Violet and I scrambled after worms big as snakes. Running around the front yard barefoot under the streetlights, we held our coffee cans tight against our bony six-year-old chests, one empty five-pound Maxwell House coffee can apiece, picking up worms that had stretched themselves out on the warm cement.

"Okay," Dad would say after about fifteen minutes into the hunt, "enough monkeying around."

This made my sister and me start going, "Oo oo oo," and scratching ourselves under our arms. Legs wide, we stuck out our bottom teeth and swung our coffee cans in front of us. "Oo oo oo," we'd go on.

Violet made a contest out of everything. Collecting bait was right up there with the best of them.

"Whoever gets the most worms gets to sit next to Dad in the Googie," she'd say.

The Googie was a pretend high-jinxer between my twin and me. He had a thing for plugging up toilets. He was also our favorite name for a bunch of stuff. Dad's small, green Googie boat had seating for the whole family: Mom, Dad, Hyacinth Suzanne, Violet and me. Mom and Hyacinth Suzanne only went out on the Googie once on account of Mom said the boat "wasn't big enough to hold a flea fart let alone a family of five, and if you and the twins want to risk your lives on this floating surfboard you'd better be wearing life jackets and carrying flares." Mom crouched like a statue, arms outstretched, both her hands gripping either side of the boat. She must have been dead serious because she never said stuff like fart. When Dad stood up and rocked the boat, Mom promised she'd get in the leaking crate again only when hell froze over.

If I collected more worms than Violet Jane, she changed it to whoever found the biggest worm. If it was me, there'd be an even better contest so that my twin never lost. And I never won. In the morning, she'd make a brand new list of contests. Violet wanted Dad to referee her feats of daring-do, but he only mussed her hair and winked at me.

"Daylight in the swamp," he'd call out from the bottom of the stairway the next morning. If we didn't answer right away, he'd pretend to talk to himself but loud enough for us to hear, "I guess I'll have to eat all these flapjacks all by myself. They're looking mighty good."

"Okay," my sister and I croaked from our sleepy beds.

"Better hurry up. These flapjacks are going fast," he'd go on. "I just might have to eat them all. All by myself."

"Nooooo!" We scampered out of our beds, racing each other into the hallway and down the stairs into the light of the kitchen where we'd find Dad standing over a hot griddle where pancakes fluffed in the pan. Spatula in hand, kitchen towel tucked into the waistband of his jeans, our father was a big, happy, smiling guy.

"Who wants the first ones?" he'd ask, as they were the most special.

"Me! Me!" We'd push through the kitchen into the breakfast nook.

"Well, who's sitting down and ready? I see two empty seats," he'd called after us.

"We're sitting down, Dad!" we both hollered, situating ourselves.

"Me first! Me first!" we begged, shooting an arm straight up overhead like we were back in Miss Johnson's kindergarten class and couldn't wait to be called on. "Me! Me! Pick me first!"

Carrying in a stack of blueberry flapjacks in a pan, Dad would dish out two plate-sized pancakes each.

"More! More!" Violet and I cried out, jittered up for the day ahead of us. We wiggled our behinds in our seats, all keyed up.

"You finish these and we'll see," he'd tease.

Quickly, my sister and I buttered our pancakes and drizzled syrup all over. Nose to the plate, we gobbled up like starving Armenians, whoever they were.

"Not too much maple syrup, now," Dad would admonish. "Don't want a belly ache. Can't catch fish if you're always squatting behind a bush."

We stopped in our tracks for a second, thinking on this last part as neither Violet nor me were keen on the no toilet thing, especially after the often told story about Aunt Sophie wiping her butt with poison ivy leaves, It was an old tale in which she'd flunked out of second grade because her behind and insides got all messed up due to the consequences of not having toilet paper while out camping with the Girl Scouts and not knowing which leaves were people friendly and which leaves were not. Three leaves! Three leaves! Three leaves! We were in a fever to learn about the three leaves after that. We burned the picture of the cluster of leaves in our brains. Don't forget about the three leaves! The adults used to laugh about it when Aunt Sophie wasn't around. Guess she didn't earn her merit badge, either. I heard it told that the itchy scabs climbed all the way up from her butt into her guts and throat and even inside her mouth. Yeesh. Just thinking about it was enough to make my hind-end itch.

But Dad's blueberry pancakes were the best. We had to eat a stack apiece. And a glass of orange juice and a glass of milk. We needed to be strong for the day ahead. There were hooks to bait and fish to catch and clean and fry. We stopped our feeding frenzy once in a while to make a muscle.

"Show me your muscles," Dad would say.

Both Violet and I would stick out our skinny chests, our six year old arms bent at the elbows, forks in fists. We gritted our teeth. We were Popeye the Sailorman. We lived in a garbage can. We ate all the worms and spit out their germs. We're Popeye the Sailorman! Toot! Toot!

"Looking good, Jack," Dad would say to me while testing my bicep with thumb and pointer finger.

"Wow, Sam," he'd say to Violet Jane doing the same thing with his big sausage fingers.

My twin and I knew it was going to be a good day when Dad used our boy nicknames.

On this particular day Dad had decided against taking the Googie out on the lake as he said it was too much monkeying around, and we'd be losing good early light getting ready. He wanted to get going before all the "horse's asses" muddied up the water with their speedboats. He said we'd do just fine if we threw our lines out from the shore.

At Carter's Bay, Violet and I helped Dad lug our gear from the Pink Swan down to the riverbank. (The Pink Swan was Dad's name for our two-toned pink and white Buick.) We labored under the weight of empty five-gallon plastic pails, rods and reels, lunch buckets, sweaters, and Maxwell House coffee cans half-filled with dirt and night crawlers big as snakes. Dad produced a red-banded "ceegar" from his breast pocket and lit up. Not allowed to smoke in the house, my father often burned through a few R.G. Dunns on our fishing expeditions. I never let on, but they sort of made me green around the gills.

"Here, Jack, hand me one of those night crawlers," Dad said, holding a barbed hook between his thumb and pointer finger while his cigar curled smoke into his eyes.

I dug around in the muck of my can for an especially large worm, one with an egg sack as they were good luck, and handed it to him. I tried not to act like a girl about it, but the squiggly thing squirreling around in my hand was creepy.

"Now move in closer so you can see how I do it," he said, clinching his teeth around his R.G. Dunn. When the hook punctured the skin of the worm, it whipped against the barb in agony.

Blueberry flapjacks rose in my throat.

"See how the hook goes right through the big middle part of the worm?" Dad instructed. "See?" He worked with it under my nose.

"Then you wrap the end around like this. Oh. Oh. He's a slippery one by cracky," he'd chuckle while piercing the poor thing again and again. Guts hung out everywhere like burst Kiska. "Then hook it again. If you can do it, hook it again so it doesn't get loose in the water. We want the fish to bite our hook, not get a free meal."

Mashed worm securely fastened and writhing, Dad was satisfied.

I nodded like everything was hunky dory. Like I was really studying the situation. Like everything was great. Like pancakes and maple syrup were not fighting in my stomach.

Handing me the rod and reel, Dad showed me once again how to cast and what to do when I got a nibble. With a small, plastic red and white bobber tied to my fishing line and floating on the water, I watched it like a hawk. Dad put Violet to rights with her gear, and then took care of his own.

The sun was already warm in the early morning hour. It was the summer of '55. Fresh marsh air rose damp in the mist. Water birds lifted off and settled back in the cattails. Comfortable, perched on bottomed-up five-gallon pails, we three huddled close together on the shoreline, warming ourselves in the sun. Safe on my own pail with Dad between my twin and me, I relaxed. With one eye on my red and white bobber and the other eye on my thoughts, it was easy to surrender into the day. I let the sun massage my shoulders and play in my hair. I let the rich aroma of the swamp invade my senses.

Thoughts of summer's end and entering first grade creeped around the edge of my musings. I watched my small bobber asleep on the water and wondered if next summer would be as good as this one. *Would we fish at Carter's Bay? Would thunderstorms make worms drop out of the sky? Would Dad let Violet and me play in the rain? Would I make new friends at school? Would learning to read be very hard?* I was surprised out of my mental wanderings when Dad tucked a loose strand of hair behind my ear.

"Angel hair," he said under his breath.

Embarrassed but proud by his attention, I grinned back before ducking away.

Without warning, a cloud dragged its cold shoulder over us. Holding tight to my rod and reel, I grabbed the edge of my pail and scooted closer to my father. When I stole a peek at Violet, I was relieved it did not look like she had seen him be nice to me. People have said that I was the "pretty one" of my twin and me. It scared me when they said things like that. Once, when Violet heard Uncle Boro tell me this, she socked me hard in the arm. Another time she kicked me with her saddle shoes. I learned to watch out for her when somebody said something about the way I looked or when something good happened.

Sitting like seagulls upon our pails, we three watched our tiny bobbers and took in the day. No one needed to make potty call, and no one needed to catch anything. Dad drank coffee from his thermos and smoked his cigars.

"Can I have a puff, Dad?" Violet asked.

"No." He took it from between his teeth to examine it. "This crummy old thing?"

"Come on, Dad?" She whined. "Just one teensy weensy little puff?"

She showed him with her thumb and pointer finger for measurement.

"Only this teensy eentsy little bit?"

He studied the chewed brown end for a moment, and said "What the hell?" and held the bundle up to her mouth so she could get a puff.

"Don't inhale," he warned.

Eagerly, Violet Jane put her mouth around the wet brown leaves, blinking against the curling smoke. She sucked in a lungful by mistake, exploding into a riot of spurts and hacks. She bolted upright and stamped her feet, ever holding on to her rod and reel.

"How'd you like it?"

Dad laughed out loud, laying his fishing gear on the ground. He thumped Violet a couple of hearty whacks on the back before offering her a sip of his coffee.

When it looked like my sister would survive her private double-dare, Dad stepped back to assess the damages.

"Are you going to make it, Sam?" He gave her a one-armed hug. "Want another puff?"

He chuckled.

"No...I don't...think so...Dad," Violet wheezed.

Dad pulled a wrinkled handkerchief from his pants' pocket and handed it to my sister. She blew her nose and gave it back. After wiping her eyes on her shirtsleeve, Violet shook her head.

"Well, I guess I'll have to check my line now that I've dropped it in the drink," Dad teased. "Fish probably been having a field day eating all our good bait."

"I got one!" I hollered and leaped from my pail, my bobber dancing crazily in the water. "I think I got a big one!"

"Hold on," Dad cautioned, setting his pole down again. He registered a glance at Violet.

"You okay?"

She nodded and snorted, tears pooling in her eyes.

"What have you got there, Jack? Remember to jerk back the line," Dad showed me in the air as if he'd got the line. "Make sure you set the hook."

"I got it! I got it!" I yelled, wrestling with my rod and reel as the great fish hauled more line out into the bay, threatening to snap my pole. Arms shaking in the effort, I planted my feet wide on the wet clay and held on for dear life.

"Hang on, Jack!" I heard Dad cheer.

Suddenly the monster jerked direction, yanking out more line. Put off balance, I sideways shuffled a couple of quick Soupy Sales moves before smacking the ground hard on my backside, sledding into the lake, all the while clutching my fishing pole.

"Hoah there!"

Dad plowed in after me, taking my rod and reel in one hand while setting me on my feet with the other hand. When the underwater giant demanded more line, we collided against each other. I jabbed an elbow into Dad's thigh, stepped on his feet, and slapped mud across his chest with the back of my hand. The jiggity-jig hit Dad's funny bone. Violet and I joined in with his belly laugh, all our sides stitching and eyes watering. We crossed our legs so as not to wet ourselves, and Violet, just newly pulled together from her coughing fit with Dad's R.G. Dunn, started hopping up and down trying to whack herself on the back with one hand while holding tight her rod and reel with the other.

Through impossible effort and several skull-jarring coughs, Dad managed to calm himself enough to pour out a bit of lukewarm coffee from his thermos. When he offered a sip to Violet, they spilled it on themselves.

"Christ!" Dad said when another ambush of giggles rendered all of us rag dolls.

Again we bent forward, hugging our sides, leaning on each other for support, only making the problem worse as syllables hissed through our teeth and tears streamed down our faces. In the fracas, Old Mr. Fish had helped himself to even more yards of fishing line.

"So you want some help with that, Jack?"

Dad blew his nose into the family handkerchief and cleared his throat.

"Christ?!" he coughed.

"I can do it," I croaked, smearing muck across my face as I wiped my eyes and nose on my shirtsleeve. Wet clay welded me to my clothes. I was a fisherman, by golly. I was Popeye the sailorman. Toot! Toot!

"I can do it!" I insisted, the pole bending abnormally in my hands. New line raced crazily across the lake.

"What a sorry sight we are!" Dad shook his head. "Christ, that was funny," he said, wiping his hand on his t-shirt. "Yoursies (Mom in Dad-talk) is not going to let us in the house after looking like a couple of drowned rats."

"Holy Toledo, Jack, you got mud all over your hind end! Going to have to hose you down when we get home." Dad scratched himself on the chin letting loose a glob of clay. "Hell, I'll have to hose myself down."

"Looks like you too, Sam."

Together, my dad and I successfully wrestled a large, prehistoric creature from the lake where it blindly flopped at our feet, smacking itself repeatedly against the clay. It opened and closed its thick lips, gulping for water like air, a popped worm dangling from its ruined mouth.

"Wow!" Dad cheered as he picked up the ancient fish by its wide gaping mouth. "Pretty good size."

He held up the thick whiskered, black-bodied animal, swinging it around for Violet to see.

"Big one, huh? Jack lands another giant of a fish. Good job."

Admiring the catch, Dad didn't see Violet stick out her tongue.

Caught up in his praise, I allowed myself a momentary bath in his warmth. When he unhooked the great fish and held it out in front of me, I took it in both my arms like it was an offering, hefting its weight. It was heavy, sticky and cold; its rubbery skin was dark as a hole. When it slapped me in the chest, I gave it back. Dad said bullheads were bottom feeders and Mom "won't have them in the house under any circumstances" since she's "eaten enough of them in her childhood to last twenty lifetimes."

Dad coaxed the beast through the water until its gills work again. All of us, Dad included, had caught our share of these dinosaurs that lived in the reeds where boats ran over them unawares. Sometimes I saw another hook in the mouth of one I'd landed and wondered how long the rusty metal had been there. *Did fish feel pain the way people do? Did worms?* When the other fishhook looked familiar, I wondered if I was catching the same tired old thing over and over again.

When Dad said we'd caught enough perch and other good eating fish, we decided to call it a day.

Carrying as much as we could in one trip, Violet and I sloshed a bucket of fish together up the hill to the waiting trunk of the Pink Swan. Dad followed close behind, loaded down with another pail of fish, his own special box of tackles, three big empty pails for sitting, two Maxwell House coffee cans half full of muck and worms, one empty thermos with screw-on cup, and two leftover cigars.

Violet and I took turns driving into town from Carter's Bay. We usually did the driving, as this was our unofficial job. We sat on

Dad's lap, seriously watching the road in front of us, both hands on the wheel, while he worked the floor pedals. Whenever we steered into the other lane, the Swan magically righted itself: Pretty good how that worked out. Violet and I started to think we were getting good as car drivers, what with all the practice we got in. On the way, Dad liked to tease us about exchanging our Mom for a couple of "spring chickens." It was one of his favorite games. Violet and I made a lot of racket about it. We said "no, no!" with feeling, and we always told Mom about it.

"Every time you and the twins come back from one of your fishing trips, we go through this nonsense. I don't find it funny in the least bit. Now come on."

The gears started turning.

"Tell you what. "I'll see if old man Gentry is available," she said, smiling to herself, knowing that our next door neighbor was about a thousand years old and equally as worn out as the other three fossils he lived with.

"Lilly June drove the Swan!" Violet chimed in.

"Yeah? Well, you smoked a ceegar," I ratted back, surprising myself.

"Honestly," Mom sighed. "If you two don't get out of my kitchen..." she threatened.

"Pete?" Now she started after Dad. "Peter, can you hear me?"

Leaving her task, she walked past us, opened the screen door, talking more to herself than to us.

"Now, where is your father?"

We knew he was in the garage but said nothing.

While standing in the doorway in search of our father, our mother came upon a new interest.

"Look at all those good apples going to waste on the ground," she said.

Violet and I scarcely breathed. No one moved. Suddenly allies, our arms taped to our sides, we were statues, hoping to become invisible, evaporating where we stood, as I was sure my sister sensed, as I did, what was next on the agenda.

"Lilly June and Violet Jane, wait a minute."

Here it comes.

But when Mom passed by us without taking notice, I thought maybe I was invisible, and started to plan big adventures with my new powers. I could....

"Take these bowls and pick up the apples that have fallen to the ground. Not the ones on the trees," Mom warned. "I think I'll bake an apple pie."

Apparently visible and command given, my sister and I slouched into the backyard, holding our heavy crockery bowls. Picking up misshapen green apples off the ground where they had had plenty of time to rot and hatch worms was a hateful task. And Mom's green apple pies were sour awful. However hard I tried, I could not manage to ever find an apple without touching something brown and soft. Sometimes I held my breath against the sharp decay. I stepped on slimy gobs of rot, trying to find an apple worth saving. When I spied Violet reaching over her head to pluck a shiny green one from the tree and put it in her bowl, I kept my head down so she didn't see that I saw her do it. I watched as she grabbed yet another flawless round apple, and still she picked another.

"Some of these apples look pretty good, like they've been picked right from the tree," Mom mused aloud, to no one in particular. "No bruises or worms. Hmm."

Examining a really green one, she said, "Glad we didn't spray for bugs this year."

***

"You missed Wagontrain," Violet said as she dropped two dimes into her glass piggy bank before throwing herself on her lower level bunk. We earned money for cutting Dad's toenails. It was a weekly event. His nails were like tree bark. We worked hard at it.

Too bad, I liked Wagontrain, I thought to myself. Using the bunk bed headboards as a ladder, I hoisted myself up to the top, unaware I'd stepped on a strand of Violet's hair.

"Ouch!"

She yanked her hair out from under my foot, pushing me off balance.

Reflexively, I tucked in my chin, cracking it against the upper bed board, biting my tongue in the process, losing my grip, and falling to the floor, my right arm bracing the fall. White-hot arrows shot out from my wrist and up my limb into my armpit. Sweat popped out all over my chest. Dots swam in front of my eyes.

When I was able to make sounds, a wail erupted from my lungs, bringing both parents into the bedroom.

"All right!" Mom shouted, "What happened?"

"Are you hurt?" Dad knelt over me on the floor. "Where are you hurt, Jack?"

Even if I could've strung some words together, my tongue was too sore to sort them out. When the mixture of blood in saliva leaked from my lips, Dad picked me up and carried me into the kitchen where the lights were brightest. He sat me down on a chair. Mom followed.

"Open your mouth, honey." Dad coaxed, his thick fingers lifting my chin.

I opened my mouth.

"Looks like you bit your tongue." He squinted. "But it's not too bad. How did you do this, Jack? Did you fall out of your bunk bed?"

"You girls need to be more careful. Maybe you should put the railing back up, Pete."

Turning to me, she said, "You could have broken your arm, falling like that---or worse."

Then she asked Violet, "Were you and Lilly misbehaving?"

"No," my sister said while looking at something in her hands.

When I favored my right arm, both parents asked me what I was doing.

I didn't want to tell them it hurt, so I sort of moved a finger.

"Hold your arm out, Jack."

"I wish you wouldn't call her Jack," Mom insisted.

I reached out, blocking the typhoon in my stomach. When heat poured over me, I blinked it back.

"Can you move your hand?" Dad wanted to know.

My head felt too big for my neck. Dark blotches twirled cross my vision.

"Looks a little peeked," were the last words I heard before swimming out of consciousness.

"Here she is," were the first words I heard when I swam back to reality. "Should we take our girl to the hospital?" It was Dad.

"Friday night? Going to be crowded." Mom said. "Lilly Jane, does your hand hurt?"

She said to Dad, "You know how Lilly faints sometimes."

"I think you should call Old Doc Meeks, Teresa. See what he says."

"I'm okay, Mom."

Fuzzy-eyed, I looked around Dad and was relieved to see that no one else had entered the kitchen. I worried that if Violet got wind of all the attention I was getting from both our parents, she'd do something, and right now I didn't feel very good.

"I feel better now." I lied.

"And my hand is okay. " More lies.

"See?" I wiggled my index finger, careful not to pass out again.

"Are you sure?" Dad searched my face.

I nodded, hoping the clanging in my forearm would soon disappear. My head pounded.

"Teresa, call Doc Meeks anyway, and see what he says," Dad insisted. "You know during the war, guys would fall into foxholes in the dark and walk for miles sometimes on a broken leg if it was a greenstick. Didn't even know they had a bum leg until they got to the medic complaining about a shin splint. Hell, I remember..."

"Peter," Mom interrupted. "Enough war stories."

"Jack---Lilly---likes my stories, don't you?"

I nodded.

"Teresa, get Doc on the phone and tell him what happened."

"You think we need to?" Mom sounded tired.

"Can't hurt."

Dad gave me a small piece of ice to suck on. He carried me into the TV room. The ice was too cold, but I didn't say so as sitting with my dad in his big chair, staying up later than we were supposed to, felt too good in spite of the pain tromping up and down in my arm. Doctor Meeks instructed my parents to watch for swelling and bruising and to call if there were any changes. He also charged them to give me half an aspirin for pain, as needed. I snuggled into my dad, relieved and grateful for his huge safety.

When Mom reported that Violet thought I slipped on the ladder, I said nothing. Mom made popcorn and stretched out on the daybed. I gummed a soft corn kernel while she and Dad and I watched the Groucho Marx Show.

When Hyacinth came home from her date, she wanted to know what I was doing up.

"Oh, she took a little tumble." Dad answered, patting my knee.

"So what happened?" Hyacinth pressed further.

"I think the twins were fooling around," Mom weighed in, her eyes on the television, "and Lilly June fell off the top bunk bed. But she seems to be on the mend."

Mom absently tossed another handful of popcorn into her mouth.

"Lilly, you fell off the top bunk?" Hyacinth seemed surprised. "And you didn't break your neck?"

"No." I shook my head, cuddled in Dad's big arms, and buried in deeper.

"Where's Violet?" Hyacinth reached for some popcorn. "In bed?"

"Uh, huh," Mom turned over. "Check to see if the light is turned off in their bedroom, will you?" Mom directed. Then to no one in particular, "I'm bushed. This has been a long week."

"Is Yoursies, tired?" Dad asked Mom.

"Yeah, Yoursies is beat," she answered. "Who's on Jack Paar tonight?"

Dad said he didn't know, but why not stay up and find out as tomorrow was Saturday, and neither one of them had to get up early.

"I'm too tired to even get up and go to bed," Mom sighed, rubbing her eyes. Accompanied by lots of moans and groans, she rolled into a sitting position, dropped her bare feet to the floor, planted her hands on her knees, and stood as if shaking off cobwebs.

"Is Yoursies going to bed?" Dad asked.

"If I can."

"Give us a kiss, then." Dad showed Mom his cheek.

"Lilly, you be careful when you climb into bed tonight."

She assessed my face. While leaning over the back of Dad's recliner, she brushed her lips past his cheek, leaving him and me alone in the quiet house. Together, we watched Jack Paar in silence except for the sounds from the television and our separate breathing. Blood had stopped trickling down my throat, my tongue ached, and my arm throbbed. I had to use the bathroom. When my dad offered me a glass of milk if I stayed up with him a little while longer, I felt blessed. When he wanted to know if I needed to use the bathroom, I was thankful. I told him I needed to go number one. I thought I could do it by myself.

In the bathroom, I struggled with my pajamas. Holding my right arm close to my chest and using my left side only, I managed to work my way out of and back into my pajama pants. Privately cradling my wounded wing with joy and lightness of spirit, I anticipated the walk through the darkened house toward life in the television room, knowing kindness and comfort awaited me in the company of my father: tall, easy-going, patient and uncomplicated. I knew I loved him and he loved me.

"How's the hand?" he asked when offering me a glass of milk. *The Honeymooners* had already started fighting without me.

"Okay. It's my arm...that hurts," I confessed, keeping the weakened limb close.

"Let me see," Dad coaxed.

"Does this hurt?" he asked, when pressing his thumb in places along my forearm.

I responded to his touch with sort of's and shrugs of the shoulder. When I winced, he apologized, and then went into the kitchen to bring back a bag of ice.

"I wonder if we should get you to the doctor."

"It's lots better with the ice," I claimed, not wanting to leave his side.

"My tongue is better already," I said, and stuck it out to show him. "See?"

He said, "Hmm."

Promise you'll let me or your mother know if your arm gets worse during the night. Or tomorrow."

I nodded that I would, hoping for tiny miracles in healing.

My eyes watched Art Carney and Jackie Gleason haggle with each other on television, but my head wandered around in the day. I remembered the taste of Dad's famous blueberry flapjacks at breakfast and the look of big old Mr. Whisker Fish after that wrestling match in the mud. I smiled around my wounded tongue, remembering the silly things we did at Carter's Bay when everyone laughed so much. When the taste of blood entered my wanderings, I pressed my cheek against Dad's chest. He patted my hair without speaking.

After the ten o'clock news, Dad gave me another half aspirin and helped me into bed. I promised I would tell him if my arm hurt in the night. He kissed me without a whisker rub and checked on Violet before leaving our bedroom. Lying on my back, I cradled my arm as if it were a tiny baby. When I tested my tongue along my teeth, I was surprised that it hurt so little. Tired from too much day and everything else, I drifted around the edges in a cloud of images, Dad's aftershave lingering on my cotton pajamas.

"What did you tell them?" Violet startled me.

I held my breath.

"What did you tell Hyacinth?"

She sounded like she was talking through her teeth.

Afraid and tired outside of myself, I remained mute. Everything hurt. I wished my dad was there.

When Violet lifted the mattress under me with her foot, the sudden shift renewed hot pokers in my arm. When she let go, my head crashed cymbals. Tears welled in my eyes, and I wished I was invisible.

Violet kicked the mattress again.

"Stop it. Please?"

Carefully placing my wounded limb across my chest, I held it in earnest, dots flashing across my eyes.

"What did you tell Mom and Dad?" She was relentless.

"Nothing."

"How come Hyacinth wanted to know what really happened?" Violet demanded.

"Mom told her I fell off the bed because we were fooling around. That's all," I told her, searching fevered memories for the earlier conversation between the two.

"It was your fault you fell," she said.

Pushing down the rise of vomit in my throat, I remained motionless and silent. When a wave of heat washed over me, I talked myself into staying alert, saying the only prayer I knew by repeating it as if it were a trusted spell:

Now I lay me down to sleep, I began in my head.

"You fell by yourself." Violet invaded my protective mantra. "Nobody pushed you. You shouldn't have let go." She sounded matter-of-fact. "If you say anything different, the bad Googie will crawl out from under the bed and get you."

I heard Violet speak about the bad Googie and registered it in a far place in my brain, making sure to keep my sister's version of the story clear in my head. I knew she would continue with it.

I had learned that the safest and fastest way to wade through her stories was to disappear. I did it then.

I imagined a long silken cord spinning out from my chest, and the real me---Lilly June/Jack---was safe, way up high overhead, while the body part of me was down on the ground, not doing or saying anything, statue-still. The real me floated in the sky for as long as I wanted. Sometimes when I was flying so high and invisible, I thought I could see other people in their houses or hear them talking to each other. I could see them. They could not see me. I did my magic trick other places too: at school or at church. Mom said I was a day-dreamer, but it was more than dreaming in the daytime. It was like I was awake, and I knew that I was in two places at the same time. Sometimes when I was sailing around like a kite in the sky, unhooked to the body of Lilly June, I felt sad for her because she had to stay and take it. I couldn't help her. I thought I would suffocate and die if I stayed on the ground or would explode into hundreds of tiny pieces of glass, never to be put right again. When I spun out, I could feel the sun without hurting. I was the air. I was a cloud. Or the rain. Or a squirrel on a wire. Sometimes I was a big and beautiful bird, wings wide, gliding with the beat of my heart, my dark velvet body making shadows over rooftops and others below. Sometimes I rested quietly atop a tall single tree, surveying my world through perfect eyes, safe at a distance.

"Everybody knows that," Violet lassoed me.

Brought back from my magical ride on eagle's wings, I could still smell his feathers and feel his heart beating. When I reached up with my mind to touch the giant bird, it whispered a single word.

"What?" I called to him.

"What?" Violet asked.

Reluctant to leave the great winged creature, I strained to know what he had said to me.

"Why did you say 'What'?"

I gave up. "Nothing, Violet."

She gave up, too.

My head spun. I cradled my beating arm and breathed deep, relieved that my sister was done talking. Done for the night. This night, anyway. I recalled my flight upon the great bird, his wings extended. I searched my mind's eye for the dark bird's voice, the feel of his feathers upon my cheek. When I remembered the peace I'd felt pressed against my dad's chest as we rocked in the big chair, I locked the perfect image into my heart, storing it with other special moments.

When the overhead light screeched through the night, I was blinded out of my pretty imaginings. My arm remembered its injury when Violet bounded out of bed under me. I heard her scuttle across the floor to the dresser where she checked its drawers, opening and closing them one at a time. She checked the closet door for possible cracks. Violet believed the bad Googie hid in the dark behind opened doors, in drawers, and under the bed. Sometimes I thought she might be right about it, even though neither one of us had ever seen him.

When Violet was satisfied with her night rituals, she tossed herself onto her bed and turned out the light in one movement, careful not to awaken the bad Googie. Anticipating her leap, I held my wounded limb so that her trouncing around wouldn't hurt as much.

But I was wrong.

With lightning bolts flashing and tears pooling, I talked to the pain. I made myself look at my mental pictures, my string of magic beads I kept safe in my heart's hope chest, and fell asleep holding each pearl.

It was while I was drowning in a night terror of bad things that Dad came into the bedroom to check on me in the night and rescued me from the attack of the giant nightmare maggots. Dazed with blinding afterimages, I was confused by his presence. Fearing the bad Googie had escaped from an unsecured hiding place, I lay frozen in sweat, my ears pounding.

"Jack," I heard Dad's voice filtered through my head horrors, his heavy hand on my forehead.

He whispered my name again. "Jack."

Pop, I realized. *Pop!* Tears poured as I was overcome with relief and joy to find him near. When I turned to face him, hot pokers jabbed in my arm.

"Jack," Dad whispered again. "I came in to check on you, and you were talking. I thought you were awake, but you must have been having a bad dream. Are you okay?"

He ran his hand over my head.

"No...I don't know." I was so relieved. "Must have been a nightmare."

I was so glad to see my pop that tears came harder.

"How's your arm?" he asked.

"Hurts a little. It's okay, though."

I didn't want to talk about my arm right now. Ugly memories of giant bug maggots stole around the corners of my brain.

"Do you need a drink of water?" he asked.

"I have to go to the bathroom."

"Can you get out of bed by yourself?"

"I think I can get down by myself."

I struggled with the headboards. Dad kept his hand around my waist while I inched my way down to the floor one-handed.

"Wait here," he said before walking to the dresser bringing back a dry pair of pajamas. "You'll have to change out of your wet ones."

We walked together though the sleeping house, streetlights illuminating familiar rooms and their contents. When we got to the bathroom, Dad turned on the light for me, and then waited outside the closed bathroom door. Using the toilet and changing my pajamas was exhausting. I braced myself against the effort, treating my arm as if it were fastened to me by a thread that could break without warning. The constant pain made me weak. I asked Dad for another aspirin before going to bed.

Safely tucked in, clean and dry, I allowed myself to drift, losing time and place, pain and monsters. I began new dreams. Good dreams. One whole day of six-and-a-half years old had come and gone.

I was glad no one told me that this was the last time I would go fishing with my dad, Pop, that it would be the last time we would ride home from Carter's Bay driving the Pink Swan, and that Violet would grow ever more confusing, and Mom more distant. That Peter Dragich, made to feel uncomfortable by his wife for encouraging his twin daughters to grow up "too much like boys," would withdraw his easy attentions, leaving his twin daughters unguided and Lilly June unprotected, except for the few locked memories she kept close, laced together like round golden beads on a silver string.

***

It was her grandmother who healed Lilly June's arm. Saturday morning, following the Friday night bunk bed accident, Mom had decided to go into the office for a few hours and picked up Baba to stay with Violet Jane and me until either Dad came home from picketing with the other strikers at Consolidated Paper Mill, or Hyacinth Suzanne came home from synchronized swimming practice. I didn't care that Violet went to play with Judy Lee Emery either, as it was a rare day in the Dragich household that I would be allowed to lie in Dad's chair unbothered, as long as I kept quiet and turned the television down low. Before leaving, Mom had put her hand on my forehead and given me half

an aspirin. When she asked how I felt, I wiggled a finger out from the towel I'd wrapped my arm in to show that it was fine. I remembered dozing most of the morning, in and out of cartoons and other Saturday shows.

When Baba walked into the television room in her rolled cotton stockings and sensible shoes, her unhurried kindness came with her. She asked me if I was hungry and why I looked white in the face.

"What's wrong with your arm?" she asked in her thick Slavic accent.

"How do you know about my arm?" I answered, looking at her curiously, as I had not said anything about it. I guessed Mom did.

"I can tell something is wrong." She watched me more keenly.

" How can you tell?"

"Look at how you hold it," she said. "And you feel weak to me."

Sometimes my Baba said strange things.

"My arm," I confessed. "Fell out of my bunk bed last night. My arm hurts."

"How did you fall out?" she asked, looking me full in the face.

"It was an accident," I answered, looking down at the towel.

"Accident?" Baba repeated.

"Where was your sister?" she asked. "What did doctor say?"

"Mom called Doctor Meeks, and he said to see if I got a bruise or if it swelled up," I answered. "I got an aspirin."

"Let me see your arm."

When Baba reached for my arm with both hands, I carefully uncovered it for her. Tears started up in my eyes again when I discovered a visible lump on my forearm, just above the wrist. It was purple. Baba said hmmm while drawing her arthritic hands over the angry swelling. Her touch felt at first hot as a poker, then cold as ice, then warm and enriching as if she were feeding my arm something whole and nutritious through her hands. My shoulders relaxed, my head cleared, my eyes stopped stinging. Suddenly, I was starving.

"How about, I make you some rice?"

Baba searched my face before letting go of my arm. Satisfied, she nodded.

"Yes, please." I nodded back at her while stretching out of the big recliner. "Rice would be good. I'm starving to death."

I stood up from my cocoon, ready to cradle my arm.

"You don't need to do that no more," she said, putting a hand on my shoulder, filling me, again, with delicious warmth that spread throughout my body in waves, making me feel full and light at the same time.

Together we walked into the kitchen where I watched Baba cook her creamy rice pudding. When I pulled a chair across the linoleum, closer to the stove so I could see better, I was surprised to find that my injured wing did not hurt at all, but rather, it felt as if it had awakened from a tingly sleepiness.

"Your arm is good now?" Baba asked when she saw me stretch it out in front, twisting my wrist to the right and then the left.

I nodded. I smiled.

"You let me know if you need help some more time." She looked me full in the eyes. "And we keep this trick with you and me, huh?"

***

And I did keep her trick with me. And forgot it until now. How did she do that with her hands? That magic. And what about fishing with Dad? And picking up worms, and driving the Pink Swan and what about the Googie? The Googie. I didn't find out the Googie was Violet Jane until I was 10 years old. Good grief.

Chapter 4.

THE MANGLER

"Thar she blows!" Violet called out as I hit the floor. "She's down for the count. Uno, dos, tres, quatro, cinco, seis."

It was the morning after the prom and the giant thinking maggots and getting my foot run over by Max Freeber. Guess you could say I was a bit under the weather--probably a lot under. Not that that was an excuse for passing out on the kitchen floor, as I was a known fainter. I had been doing it pretty regular since I was a kid.

"You're like one of those goats in *National Geographic*," Violet said after I came to. "Any little thing and boom you're out. Maybe you've got a brain tumor." She paused. "Es muy posible."

I raised my hands to my face and was relieved to see my nails were not painted blue, green or yellow, and there were no magic marker tattoos down my arms. I ran a hand through my hair and breathed a sigh when nothing sticky or powdery came off. Fainting in front of Violet or falling asleep before she did could be hazardous to my health. After I checked out okay, I asked, "Isn't that cancer?"

"If it was cancer, you'd've been dead by now since you've only been blacking out everywhere, what? Since kindergarten?" Violet said. "Must be the benign kind that just sits around in your head forever but doesn't kill you. There are those kinds of tumors, you know. Don't you remember old Mrs. Kellogg telling us about benign tumors in health class?"

Not really. I must have been cruising around the galaxy that day.

Violet went on, "I saw a picture of a woman in *National Enquirer* at Barb's house who had a tumor the size of a basketball hanging off her neck. Supposed to be some kind of a goiter that went haywire. It didn't hurt, I guess, but it was sure ugly looking."

"Didn't Baba have a goiter?" I asked, sitting up and taking the washcloth off my forehead. I crab-scooted to the cabinet doors for support.

"You mean that bump she had in the front of her neck?" Violet asked. "Mom said it was from not getting enough iodized salt. Hell, I thought that's the only kind of salt you could get was eye-o-dized. Maybe it was a leftover from the Old Country when she was a kid or something."

"Maybe." I started to feel sweaty.

"You look *muy crapolita*," Violet said. "Maybe you better lie down again and put your feet up *para uno minuto*."

"I'm okay."

"What the hell?" Violet said, looking around. "Shouldn't someone be taking you to the hospital and getting your brain x-rayed? You're always fainting. It could be something!"

I heard my sister talking through the fog in my head but couldn't get anything to work up there. I heard her say something about breathing, so I did. The air cleared.

"I bet if this was Barb's house, her mom would've carted her off to the hospital, no ifs ands or buts about it," Violet said.

"I'm feeling better, really." I hoped. "Don't get Mom. She's busy."

"She's always busy, a regular Speedy Gonzales."

"She isn't in the best mood when she's got to take care of us."

"Yeah, I noticed like when we're coughing and hacking we still got to go to school." Violet thought about it. "Barb gets to stay home if she gets a hangnail. Hell, she's always missing school for something."

I leaned into my foot and tried to work the stained cotton anklet away from my heel. It was stuck.

"Yuck," Violet said as I carefully inched the stiff sock over the heel of my foot.

I fought back the dots. I breathed and sweated.

"Huh?" Violet said when she saw my uncovered foot. "I thought it would look all bloody and deformed with bones sticking out? *Muy grossito*."

I braced myself. It looked like a scab had grown over the run over part and had shrunk to the size of a half dollar. . How is that? I touched it with my pointer finger and it felt hard. It didn't hurt, either. Pretty weird.

"How'd that mess heal up so fast?" Violet studied the situation. "I'd've thought you'd be crippled up. Broken foot. Need a crutch. A good hollering from Mom, anyway." She paused. "Looks like you might get away with it. You're *una* lucky *muchacha*."

I rolled onto my knees and held onto the counter top for support. I stood up, putting equal pressure on both my feet. No sweating. No dots. I tried walking around without holding on to anything. I was doing it. Look at that? I was going to be okay. Sort of reminded me of when Baba fixed my arm when I was a kid. Pretty good. I moved my foot to the right and then to the left. I wiggled my ankle around and around.

"I don't get it," Violet said, scratching her head, "*no lo conprende.*"

"You don't get what?" Mom asked, entering the kitchen from the basement steps.

"Lilly messed up her foot last night getting out of Freeber's dad's car, and it's almost all better. It shouldn't be," Violet said. "Should've broken a bone. It was mangled *muy mal.* Looked like a skinned tomato."

"Let me see," Mom ordered, looking down at my foot.

I balled up the dirty sock in my hand behind my back and lifted up my cotton pajama pants leg. I stood on my good foot and turned the other around so she could see it better.

"There's no discoloration," Mom said, adjusting her glasses. "This is an old scab. Couldn't have gotten this hardened overnight."

She tapped it with her fingernail. "When did this happen?" Last night?"

Then she said, "How?" and let go of my foot. She waited for an answer.

"I guess I got out of the car before Charlie's dad stopped." I didn't want to say more than I had to.

"You didn't wait for Charles to open the door for you?" Mom asked. "I thought we talked about letting him open the door for you."

"I guess I got nervous about it."

"Yeah, he was going to kiss her," Violet chimed in, happy with herself.

Mom looked at me. Waiting.

I waited, too.

Pretty soon we both stopped waiting and she said, "Have you girls eaten yet? It's getting late, and you're still in your pajamas. There's work to do. You've got your Saturday chores ahead of you," she said. "I'm downstairs ironing."

"*En la mangle?*" Violet wanted to know.

Both Violet and I got hypnotized watching Mom work her mangle iron. It had knee pedals and a huge roller that gobbled up the wrinkled material she fed it, leaving pressed clothes in a layered wrap on the other side. Steam billowed out when she lifted the scorched roller top.

Mom was an ironing maniac. Once in a while she'd let Violet and me run a pillowcase through the presser or one of Dad's hankies. It was scary how shirts and stuff got sucked in and flattened like a pancake. We had to keep watching our fingers when we ironed so as not to get sidetracked and burn ourselves flat. I had to sit on my imagination when I mangled.

"If we hurry up and eat, can we come down and watch you iron?" Violet asked. She was just about dancing in place.

"Can we?" I asked, no longer sick.

"If you get going. I'm in the middle of it right now. I want to finish before your father gets home," Mom said, getting a glass of water from the tap and drinking in a full swallow.

"I want to hear about this kiss," she said, looking at me.

Violet Jane and I had ourselves flanking Mom. We perched on stools dragged over from the wet bar.

"Why do we have a bar if no one ever uses it?" Violet asked Mom.

"Because it came with the house. It was already here."

In front of our eyes a tablecloth had been transformed from a wrinkled rag into a piece of pressed art. Her knee to the side pedals, steam billowing, Mom rearranged the cotton and lace cloth. Pedal engaged, roller top down, she fed the hungry beast. Violet and I could not pull our eyes away from Mom and her machine. She was an iron tamer.

We hardly ever got to hang out with Mom. Violet and I mostly steered clear of her because by eighth grade, getting into her sights meant she'd found some extra hateful thing for us to do after our regular chores. Mom wasn't much of a hang-arounder. I guess no one else was allowed to hang around, either.

We watched, transfixed, while Mom whipped clothes into shape. I think she got hypnotized too, since everybody stopped talking for a while.

"So, Lilly, how was the dance?" Mom finally asked, encased in a cloud of steam. "You and Charles looked so grown-up in your formal attire."

You mean monkey suit. "Okay. Charlie Freeber was still big and sweaty. So's his dad. What's his mom look like?" I was still wondering about their heads.

"Charlie always looks like he's just run a marathon," Violet added.

"Shirley's a pretty girl," Mom said, ignoring Violet. "Slight build. Petite."

She picked up another wrinkled thing from the damped pile in the wicker basket.

"So I'll bet you looked as pretty as the other girls in your gown and pumps." Mom smiled. "Both of you looked like mature young ladies."

Violet and I rolled our eyes. We hated it when Mom said mature. She pronounced it "ma-too-er." I hoped she wasn't going to bring up our periods as talk of them usually followed a ma-too-er-ity discourse. Geez.

"Your first pair of heels," Mom said wistfully. "Hope they'll last a while."

"Lilly's are messed up on account of Max Freeber's *muy grande* automobile ran over her foot," Violet reminded Mom.

"Only one shoe," I mumbled.

"Well, you can't walk around with only one good shoe," Mom said, folding something in her lap. "I'll take a look at it. Lilly, I can't believe he ran over your foot," she said. "You should have told your father and me about it last night."

"It was late," I said, slouching on my perch. "Violet helped me out."

"Yeah, I got her peroxide and bandages and stuff," Violet said, turning around on her stool. "And an aspirin. She was okay, except when she fainted in the kitchen, again."

"Lilly?" Mom looked at me. "You fainted? Were you having one of your migraines? You could have hurt yourself."

"It wasn't a migraine," I said. *Violet's always tattling, darn it.*

"Migraines are hard. I used to get them when I was ma-too-ering, too," Mom said. She ironed something as if she was working at origami.

"That was nice of you, to help your sister, Violet. But both of you should have still told us."

My twin and I looked at each other. We were okay handling stuff on our own as we'd been handling stuff on our own since we were kids. We were sort of a subgroup inside the family unit. We are known as The Twins most of the time as in, Where are The Twins? or Are The Twins ready yet? or What are The Twins up to? or You Twins are going to be the death of me.

"So did you enjoy yourself too, Violet?" Mom asked.

"Sure. There were a bunch of us guys who went with friends. Probably more people went with friends than dates," Violet said.

I didn't agree but wasn't ready for an argument.

"Lilly puked up punch down the front of her dress in the gym," she said. "I helped her clean up in the bathroom."

"Lilly?" Mom scrunched her eyebrows at me.

"Went down the wrong pipe," I answered and hoped it would be the end of the conversation.

"Yeah," Violet said. "I heard Charlie said Lilly had *muy* sexy legs."

Mom stopped her mangling.

"Sounds like junior takes after his as quickly as you did." She picked up another damp scrap. "You two have to be more careful."

Back to The Twins thing again as if Violet and I were both run over.

Chapter 5.

MIGRAINES AND MR. JONES

In our house, being sick was a drag for everybody concerned. In kindergarten, I had a problem with needles and routinely fainted while waiting in line for my polio shot. I got to where I was able to call out to whoever was standing behind me that I was going down. Sometimes I was lucky enough to get caught before I hit the ground; other times, I ricocheted around like a Ping-Pong ball between the wall and drinking fountain and floor. I imagine I hit a few classmates who got in the way. When I started getting migraines in sixth and seventh grade, I held out for as long as I could, usually waiting until I was blind and puking and falling out of my chair. Once, I had a migraine in church and two old men carried me down the aisle like I was a sack of potatoes. One old guy had my arms and the other old guy had my legs, and they sort of hammocked me back and forth while they hauled me out of St. John's Episcopal Church, my dress flapping in the breeze, showing my cotton underwear to all interested parties. My knights in shining armor set me outside on the front steps "for air" while they smoked a couple of cigarettes. I don't think I had any holes in my underpants that time.

Another time I got a migraine and fainted at flag raising at 4-H Camp. The night before I'd slept something terrible. I fainted in the middle of the Pledge of Allegiance. I wasn't all the way out, as I remembered Counselor Rick picking me up and carrying me like I was a damsel in distress and not like a sack of food. He carried me in his arms all the way to the nurse's cabin, which would've been cool if I wasn't blotto. I had my eyes cracked open and saw what was going on in front of me but couldn't get my brain to work. (Maybe I do have a tumor that hangs around in my head forever but doesn't kill me.) Mom had to drive up from Custer and take me to the doctor's office in a nearby town. I had to drink orange flavored medicine three times a day and stay out of the water for a week. The doctor said my problem was hormones, which was supposed to answer everything. I guess it did for Mom. I must've been ma-too-er-ing. Violet and I stayed on another week, giving me enough time to get a crush on Counselor Rick, go swimming, do handicrafts, swat mosquitoes, step on spiders and eat snotty oatmeal for breakfast along with everyone else.

Once I got a migraine in the movies and did not pass out. Violet and Barb and I went to see *Tom Jones*. I liked the strangely erotic part about Tom Jones and his girlfriend eating fried chicken. They had grease dripping down their arms and into their clothes and didn't care. They ate chicken while sitting together in a horse drawn carriage and laughed when they went over bumps in the road. They ate with their mouths open and kissed each other with grease across their faces. I didn't know chicken could be so good. When Violet told Mom about the fried chicken part, Mom's eyebrows went up as she said she thought Tom Jones was some kind of an historical film. I guess there was some history in it, but I don't remember much else as I got caught up trying to see around my migraine and the chicken thing. I have eaten fried chicken since, but never got the hang of it like Mr. Jones and his girlfriend.

Dad used to make me fried bologna sandwiches he cut in half and brought to me on a plate in his and Mom's bed with the curtains drawn when I was lucky enough to get a migraine and pass out and throw up while he was home from work. Mom always came to get me from the nurse's office, regardless of who watched me later. She'd have to take off work and drive me home from school. I usually smelled of vomit and my head felt like it had burst open. My blind eyes burned, and my stomach was a sloshing bucket of bile. When I was a kid, Bobby Upstairs (this is what Violet and I called him because he lived in the duplex upstairs from us) stuck a stick in my eye. I never saw right after that. Sometimes I knew a migraine was coming on if I slept badly the night before, or if I caught the sun shining on a chrome bumper of a car on the way to school. I knew that afterimage spot was going to spread into a blind aluminum half moon in my left field of vision. I never said anything while it was going on and did a lot of hoping and checking. By the time I got through an hour of school, I was puking and blacked out on the floor of somebody's classroom. I probably should have told someone ahead of time, but that meant Mom would have to call in to work if Dad wasn't home, or she'd have to run to get Baba when Baba was still alive. It was always a hassle, any way you looked at it. I tried my best to pretend I was okay until the puking part gave me away.

Chapter 6.
MYSTICS AND
MISDEMEANERS

"She said the place was haunted. She said Jeda was all over her. She said he used to climb up the stairs at night, thud, thud, thud *en los muy grande zapatos*," Violet said. "And crawled right up on top of her while she slept. Right on top of her! What the hell is that? I'd've crapped my pants. All she did was pull the covers over her head. *Es muy stupido*."

"How come you have to talk Mexican all the time?" Boo said.

"It's cultural," Violet said. "And it's not Mexican, it's Castilian, Senior Madrias said. But what about Jeda's ghost?!"

"Get out," Boo said. "I don't believe you about Jeda's ghost."

"Who said about Jeda's ghost?" I said.

"I heard her tell Mom. It's why she moved out," Violet said.

"Get out," Boo said.

"Christ, Boo, if you don't believe me, ask your mom. She'd know if our mom knows since that's why we're all back at Baba's house, fixing it up to sell."

"I didn't know," I said.

"You never know anything, Lilly," Violet said, making a face. "You're always on Mars."

Nearly two years had passed since our grandmother's burial and wake. She'd taken an elderly Polish widow in to share expenses. Probably to keep an eye on each other since both of them were getting up in years. After Baba died, the family allowed Mrs. Wozjec to stay on alone in the house until her own people figured out what to do with her. I guess she got tired of all the ghosts lying on top of her.

The relatives decided it was time to sell anyway, so Mom organized the aunts and uncles and cousins for a long weekend and had everybody's role mapped out. The men folk were in charge of building and hammering and sawing things, while the women and girls washed walls and dusted and cleaned out rooms. It had been a couple of years since some of us had been together, and we were all getting into the swing of things. And the upstairs bedrooms and attic might have had something even more interesting than usual going on since the scandal with old Mrs. Wozjec and Grandpa's ghost.

"I'd've had a heart attack if Jeda's ghost would've laid on top of me," I said. "In the dark. Just gives me the crawlies thinking about it."

"I know I'd've shit my pants," Violet said.

"Me, too," Boo said. "Honestly, Violet, you swear like a truck driver. Does your mom know how much you swear? My mom would've had a bar of soap in my mouth a thousand times by now."

"Violet watches out for the folks," I answered for my sister.

"Yeah, I'm careful, pretty much," Violet said. "Got caught once saying crap and got my face slapped. I mean is crap swearing? Of course, Dad swears all the time. I think he makes up some of the words he uses since I haven't heard them anywhere else. Of course, how would I? I mean everyone's pretty careful around us 'little pictures.' When do we start being big pictures?"

"When we ma-too-er." I laughed. Boo and Violet laughed, too.

"Let's ask our moms about why old Mrs. Wozjec moved out. Let's ask about Jeda's ghost being on top of her," Boo said. "Maybe she was just off her rocker like Aunt Beulah. Maybe there's more ghost stories."

"Yeah, like when Baba stuck a knife in the door to keep the evil spirits from getting Uncle Sava," I said.

"Yeah, like when Jeda's grandpa got his head chopped off for having sex with the farmer's wife," Violet said.

"Yeah," we all said together and jumped up in search of our mothers.

Chapter 7.

MORE MYSTICS AND WRONG DOINGS

"What's she doing here?" Violet and Boo and I whispered to each other.

We were clumped together at the bottom of the stairs when we saw Cousin Julia in a print cotton dress, sitting spread eagle on the couch, rolling a cigarette. We skirted around her on our way to find our mothers, afraid something of hers would jump off onto us. Details were hard to come by, but legend had it that Cousin Julia was the most beautiful girl at school, smart and popular, until she had her appendix operated on and caught schizophrenia. Mom said it was on account of the anesthetic. Cousin Julia was fifteen at the time, and now she was thirty and fat. She lived in a mental institution. She did not say much, and she wore dark circles around her eyes like a raccoon. Sometimes she wrote letters to Mom that never made it out of the year she caught schizophrenia. Sometimes she got a day pass and Uncle Drugo and Aunt Mara brought her to Baba's house to be around real people.

"Mom, what's Crazy Julia doing here?" Violet asked. Mom was in the kitchen with Aunt Sophie, stacking pots and pans on the table. "*Es muy loca.*"

"She's visiting her family," Aunt Sophie said. "Now be nice. She can't help it."

"Where's her parents?" Cousin Boo asked.

"Just Uncle Drugo's here. He's outside fixing the fence with your father and the twins' father."

"Did they find any golf balls?" Boo asked hopefully.

"I think your father's got a pail with him. Why don't you run outside and see?" Aunt Sophie told Boo.

We scrambled out of the house into the back yard in search of our fathers and the pail. Our grandparents had bought a house that butted up to a country club with a golf course. Baba's back yard caught golf balls regularly. When Jeda was alive, no golfers dared brave the fence to collect their little white balls as Jeda'd give them a fist and a hollering. Most of the time, none of the golfers knew if he was dead or alive, so Baba's yard stayed peppered with little white balls. Boo's dad was a weekend golfer and picked up free foul balls in Baba's yard. When we got to Uncle Tony, he had almost a full bucket of balls.

"Wow," we three cousins said, peering into the pail as if we were looking at Easter eggs from a hunt.

"Did you get all of them, Daddy?" Boo wanted to know.

"I think there's still a few the other side of the property line, Pumpkin," Uncle Tony said.

We raced around the boundary lines between the golf course and Baba's backyard. We each found a couple of handfuls of the small pocked balls. Uncle Tony and Dad called us back when they found us on the other side of the fence, walking up to the ninth hole green where the grass was like a stainless carpet. The closely mowed grass held my twin and I fascinated. We couldn't figure out how grass got like this. What kind of grass was it? How could anyone cut it this close? With what? And why? It looked and felt like someone's buzzed brush hair cut. Sometimes, when no one was looking, Violet and I would lay down on the ninth hole green, hands folded behind our heads like we were at home watching TV. Like we were laying inside our house on the floor with the sky for our ceiling, making animals out of the clouds. We never stayed long as we feared getting conked on the head by a ball or, at least, run off by the golf course police.

When Hyacinth Suzanne and some of the older cousins walked back from the corner store, loaded down with cold ham, roast beef and lamb, sliced cheese, crunchy vegetables and dip, sweet and dill pickles, Coke and Vernors, plain and barbequed chips, pumpernickel, rye, and regular bread---and a double layer chocolate cake with buttercream chocolate frosting and a gallon of milk--adults and kids alike threw down whatever they were holding and made a bee line for the house and kitchen. Mom and Aunt Sophie tried to organize a buffet at the living room table, complete with paper plates and napkins, but it turned into a mad house anyway. Violet, Boo and I danced around on the edge of the feeding frenzy like we had to use the bathroom, waiting for our turn to get at the cornucopia. The men folk filled up their plates first, then the older kids, then the Moms, who sampled everything while they brought trays to the table, and then us youngsters and any other stragglers-on. Somebody helped Crazy Julia, who ate with her mouth open and held her sandwich between nicotine stained fingers from all those cigarettes she liked to roll. It was hard to eat with her around, and I was relieved to have been sent outside with Boo and Violet to eat our sandwiches and trimmings out on the back porch steps. It was kind of a great day, when I thought about it: warm, sunny, but not too hot. Lots of okay stuff to do with lots of okay people. It was a different kind of a day than the usual fare of Saturday chores and Violet's crabbiness. I liked most of the relatives that came together for the work weekend, even if there were chores to do. There was plenty of help if anyone needed it. Hyacinth and other older cousins did some of the junk work that our parents wouldn't let Boo or Violet or me tackle, like dragging out Baba's big wool living room rug and throwing it over the clothes line to beat the crap out of it with a broom. Hyacinth and Cousin Danitsa and Bob worked up a sweat hauling that thing out of the house and up over the line. They even let each of us have a whack at it with the broom. We pretended it was a *muy grande pinata.*

When the fence got fixed, Dad outfitted me and Violet with brushes and paint.

"Your hands are small," he said. "You two monkeys can reach in between the slats better than me and Uncle Tony."

"You can help, too," Uncle Tony told Boo. "You start scraping so the twins can paint."

And he gave her a scraper to which she rolled her eyes so he couldn't see, as nobody liked scraping. Ever. I'd rather deal with the gasoline or turpentine wash after painting than scraping any day, even if the fumes sometimes burned my eyes and made me puky.

Violet and I knew the drill, as we'd been painting our own porch and railings and the garage regularly since we were kids. Dad even rigged up a scaffolding last year so my twin and I could get to the second story windows of our house. Mom found out when she came home from work, and nobody broke their necks, but Dad got yelled at anyway. Violet and I thought we were pretty cool, hoisted up on the boards and ropes hanging off the house. We even had a bucket rigged to haul up supplies like peanut butter and jelly sandwiches and pop and chips and stuff.

"So how come Wilson and Uncle Milan and Aunt Carol aren't here?" Boo wanted to know. She was scraping a couple of slats in front of me and Violet. We were sitting on the ground with our legs crossed.

"Mom said it was too far to come for only a weekend," Violet said, liberally slathering white paint up and down a board.

"I heard Mom and Aunt Beulah talking about Cousin Debbie got brainwashed in a religious cult out there in California," I said, painting the other side of Violet's board.

"When did they say that?" Violet said, staring at me through the slats. She jabbed the hard end of her brush into my hand.

"Really?" Boo said stopped in mid-scrape.

"You never know anything, Lilly," Violet said. "How the hell did you find that out and I didn't? You never pay attention to anything besides your crummy TV shows that you watch all day, let alone something like this."

Violet attacked a fence board, slapping paint on my fingers and up my arm.

"I don't believe you."

"Violet, watch where you're painting!" Boo said, stopping her scraping. "You're mean to Lilly."

"It's okay," I said, dragging my brush up and down the board like I was okay, as if not changing what I was doing would keep me held together.

"I think you're mean," Boo insisted.

"What do you know?" Violet shot back to Boo. "Mind your own beeswax." "You're always picking on Lilly."

"It's okay," I said, hoping to keep Violet off Boo while trying to see the board in front of me through eyes that were filling up.

"You're going to hurt Lilly's feelings." Boo said.

"Her feelings are always getting hurt," Violet said. "She's such a baby."

"No, she's not," Boo said, still not scraping. "She's the same age as you."

"She's a stupid candy ass dumb blonde."

"No, she's not," Boo said, forgetting her own hair was curly blond. "Lilly makes good grades in school."

"I'm not talking about school. Who gives a rat's ass buttwipe about school?" Violet said. "You don't live with her. She's always following me around. I can never get away from her. She's like a booger on my finger I can't shake off. Everywhere I go, there she is, like a bad stink."

None of what Violet said was new to me as I'd sort of heard it before. Regularly. I wished Boo would stop talking. I prayed my sister wouldn't turn on her too, as Violet's moods could change in a flash. As a practice, she bit only when we were alone. Snot hung from my nose, but I didn't wipe it. I kept my head down and painted like I was okay, not even talking to myself in my head.

"You're supposed to get along." Boo got up on her knees. "You're twin sisters! You're born at the very same time, for pity's sake!"

"Like that's supposed to mean something?" Violet geared up, ignoring Boo and me on the other side of the fence. "Yeah, like it's supposed to mean something," Boo went on. "I'd give my eye teeth to have a sister."

"Yeah, well, why don't you take her then?" Violet hissed. "Go on!"

"Well, maybe I will," Boo shot back.

"Yeah?" Violet spit.

"Yeah!" Boo spit back.

Pretty soon, white paint was in the air. Boo and Violet were both standing up, hollering at each other across the picket fence,

Boo with her scraper pointing and Violet with her brush splattering. I was sort of hunkered down behind the slats, trying to be invisible, waiting for the dust to clear, which didn't take all that long since Dad and Uncle Tony intervened pretty quick. They'd been having a beer on the back porch steps watching us the whole time we'd been scraping and painting.

"Hold your horses!"

Dad stepped over the fence, pulling Violet away from Boo. He took her paintbrush. And I took the time to wipe my face on my sleeve.

"What's going on down here?" Uncle Tony asked.

Boo and Violet looked at each other and breathed hard.

"I'm waiting," Uncle Tony said to Boo.

"Nothing," Boo said.

"Doesn't look like nothing to me," Uncle Tony said. "You've got paint in your hair."

"Lilly, what's this all about?" I felt Dad's eyes on me as I was still sitting on the ground, painting, not looking at anyone.

"It was about that I heard Wilson's sister Debbie got brainwashed into a religious cult in California." I cleared my throat and took a deep breath.

Dad raised his eyebrows. So did Uncle Tony. They both said, "Hmmm."

"That's what the ruckus is about?" Dad asked.

"She said Lilly was stupid and a buttwipe and a dumb blonde and that she didn't know anything. Then I said that she got good grades in school." Boo glared at Violet. "And that she is mean."

"All right, that's enough." Uncle Tony said to Boo and took her by the arm and led her away.

"Your mouth is going to get you into real trouble someday, young lady," Dad said to Violet who was back sitting on the ground painting again, acting like he hadn't warned her about anything. "Do you two think you can finish painting the rest of this without getting riled up?"

We both shrugged where we sat.

"What's wrong with you two?" Dad asked. "You used to get along real good."

I'd just started to breathe right again. I didn't say anything, as I was trying to be as small as possible without disappearing. I wondered where he'd been all these years.

"I'll scrape. There's only a little left to do."

Dad groaned, got down on his hands and knees, and said Christ. After a while, Violet asked him about Cousin Debbie and the religious cult. He told her to stop monkeying around and to ask our mother.

"Mom!"

Violet elbowed me as we raced up the steps into the kitchen, still dripping water off ourselves from the outside spigot where we'd taken turns washing off the gasoline from our arms and hands. Boo was already helping to wrap plates and stuff from the cupboards. Violet said oh when she saw her sitting between our moms.

"Grace says you two were fighting outside," Mom said to me and Violet. "Honestly, you two are a handful, lately."

"Not Lilly," Boo said, wrapping newspaper around a dessert plate.

"Lilly said that Cousin Debbie got brainwashed into a religious cult in California and that's why Uncle Milan and Aunt Carol didn't come to help for the weekend," Violet said.

"Well, that's not the reason," Mom said, pressing her lips together and putting a wrapped plate into a large box. "It's too far for them to come all this way for only a few days."

"What about the brainwashing part?" Violet wanted to know. "Is that part true? Did Cousin Debbie get her head reprogrammed?"

Mom looked at Aunt Sophie.

"There was talk about your cousin getting involved with a group of people who were telling her things about the Bible that your Uncle Milan and Aunt Carol didn't agree with," Aunt Sophie said.

"So what happened?" Violet asked.

"I guess Debbie's parents did an intervention," Aunt Sophie said, handing a plate to Mom.

"What's that?" Boo asked.

"Debbie's parents went to where she was staying and brought her home," Aunt Sophie said. "Your cousin didn't want to leave. She was confused."

"Like, they kidnapped her?"

Violet leaned her elbows on the table while her feet danced around underneath. Her eyes sparkled in hopes of a new tidbit to catalogue in her mental book of weird stuff.

"I read in the *National Enquirer* about how people get their brains scrambled up by the Harry Criscos. They give up all their inheritance to the Harry Criscos and live on a farm with no toilets. And everyone runs around in a dress. Even the guys. They sing about Harry Crisco all the time. And give people flowers."

Mom said something about Barb's mother and her silly magazines.

"Aunt Amelia brings over the same ones," Violet said.

"Well, whomever has them, they are trash, and I don't want you two reading them."

Mom handed a plate to Boo.

"So Uncle Milan and Aunt Carol stayed home to watch Cousin Debbie?" I asked. "So she won't run away, again? And join a farm with no toilets and where people sing about this Crisco guy and wear dresses?" I thought a second. "California sounds weird."

"Edge of the world," Mom said.

"Teresa," Aunt Sophie said.

Chapter 8.

LEGENDS, BIRDBATS AND BARE-NAKED BUTTS

"Violet got pretty worked up when we were down by the fence," Cousin Boo said when Violet left the room where we were washing windows to go to the bathroom. "Is she still so mean to you?"

"I think she didn't like it that I knew something about Cousin Wilson, and she didn't," I said. "I think she's got a crush on him. Wonder if they kissed or something when they were out behind the barn at Baba's funeral last time Wilson was here."

"He's our cousin!"

Boo was scandalized.

"My cousin on my dad's side, Pete Dragich, from Iowa, and I had a crush on each other when we went to visit them last summer." I dunked my rag in the bucket of vinegar and warm water. "I thought he was cool."

"Can't you get arrested for that?" Boo said, folding her dry rag in her lap.

"You can't get arrested for liking people. Liking is in your head or heart. You don't get arrested for just thinking about stuff. Not that I know of. People can't know what you're thinking. That's mind reading, and I don't know of anyone who can do that. Maybe on TV or in the movies," I said, "but not for real."

Sometimes I wondered about my twin and me. Sometimes I knew she was angry with me when I wasn't even around, but I didn't tell Boo.

"Yeah, but it usually leads to them doing something," Boo pressed on. "Like kissing, and that's got to be against the law." She worked at a spot on the glass.

"What's against the law?"

Violet was back.

"Kissing your cousin," Boo said.

"What cousin? What are you guys talking about now?"

Violet picked up a rag and dunked it in the bucket.

"Lilly said people can't get arrested for liking their cousins, and I said I thought it was against the law, and Lilly said thinking isn't against the law, and then I said if people think about liking someone, they usually do something about it, like kissing, and I thought kissing your cousin was against the law."

Boo got it all out pretty close to what we'd said.

"And then Lilly thought you got worked up about Cousin Wilson's older sister, Debbie, because she thought you and Wilson had a crush on each other, and she wondered if you two kissed behind the barn at Baba's funeral."

Violet drew in a breath. She let it out, and I could see the gears going around. She didn't sock me in the arm, but I didn't relax either.

"What makes you think anything happened?" was what Violet ended up saying, her eyes dark.

I stepped away.

"I don't know. It was Lilly who said it."

Boo was not helping the situation.

"I said that Cousin Pete and I had a crush on each other last summer when we went to Iowa," I said, detouring the conversation. "He was nice."

"I thought Cousin Joey was *mas simpatico*," Violet said, washing a window. "Mom about had a heart attack when Aunt Pamela said that first cousins used to get married all the time." Violet snickered. "We were supposed to stay a whole week but we left *manna por la manna*."

"I never heard of first cousins getting married," Boo said.

"Boo, you're about as dense as they come."

I could see Violet sorting through her mental filing cabinet. She was getting ready to illuminate us common folk with her expertise.

"Mr. Bartlett said in World History that most of the nobility in Europe married their first cousins to keep royal blood *en la familia* which is why some of them were *muy loco in la cabesa*. He said that story about Cinderella and her wicked stepmother and stepsisters was to keep the peasants in line. And that fairytales were originally made for adults, not kids. He said Walt Disney changed everything to make it more palatable for kids since he turned it into a cartoon, and that the real stories were gory like the stepsisters cutting off parts of their feet and stuff to get them in the glass slipper."

Violet stopped to get her breath.

"I sort of remember him talking about that," I agreed.

"Why did Walt Disney change it?" Boo asked.

"Probably *para mas grande dinero*," Violet said, dunking her rag.

Boo took a moment as maybe she was sorting through Violet's Spanish.

"So Walt Disney changed *Snow White and the Seven Dwarves*, too? And Bambi?"

I could see she didn't want to believe it

"*Bambi?*" Violet said. "*Bambi* wasn't a fairytale. *Bambi* was a cartoon."

Outside, a big Cadillac turned into Baba's driveway, dragging a trailer behind it. We three went to the window in time to see Aunt Lottie and her girlfriend get out of the car. Aunt Lottie's real name was Lubliana, which I thought was real pretty, but a long time ago nobody could spell it. Aunt Lottie was born in the Old Country; so was Uncle Drugo. They had to wait for Grandpa Jeda to earn enough money to send for them after he came to America to work. He went across the Atlantic Ocean in a big ship like the Titanic, only at the bottom of the boat where poor foreigners and animals traveled like slaves, Mom said. Aunt Lottie and Uncle Drugo were kids when they arrived in The States. They went with Baba across the ocean like slaves, too. Mom said most foreigners did. Then they got processed at Ellis Island in New York where everyone's names got messed up. Aunt Lottie got married when she was still a teenager, but he ran off before I was born. They sold bootleg whiskey from Canada with other Serbians, drove cars without a license, bet on everything, gambled with everything, smoked big cigars, burned their house down and had three kids in Custer, Michigan, before she caught cancer and took up with Ester.

Aunt Lottie had black hair cut short and greased back. She wore white anklets and sensible nun's shoes like Baba. I never saw her in anything but a white short-sleeved shirt and navy blue pants. Ester, on the other hand, was all red hair piled high, red lipstick, red lacquered fingernails and toenails, red print blouse and red Capri stretch pants. She wore open-toed high-heel shoes without any backs on them. Aunt Lottie smoked unfiltered cigarettes she held between her teeth that she learned to smoke while she was "doing time." Ester smoked hers stuck into a long pearl-handled stick. It was hard not to stare at Ester. She looked like she should've been in the movies.

Aunt Lottie and Ester had been coming to Baba's house for as long as I can remember. Mom said they were roommates and that Aunt Lottie was finally happy, that whatever she wanted to do was her business, and that Ester was not what we were used to, but good company for Aunt Lottie. Don't make judgments.

"She's a dyke," Violet said, as we watched Aunt Lottie and her girlfriend climb out of their Cadillac. I could hear Ester's high heels clacking around on the driveway below.

"What's a dyke?" Boo wanted to know.

"Christ, Boo, you'd think you were five years younger instead of only one," Violet said. "A dyke is a lesbian. A girl who likes other girls."

"What's wrong with that? I like my friend Susie Goodrow?"

"Do you want to kiss her?"

"Kiss her?"

"Yeah, lesbians kiss other girls like they're a boy," Violet said.

"Get out," Boo said.

"Get out nothing," Violet said.

"She's always nice to me," I said.

Wondering about the kissing part. Wondering why anyone would want to kiss another girl like it was a guy. I thought Ester was cool and all, like Miss Kitty on Gunsmoke, but I couldn't get my mind around the kissing part. I never even kissed a boy yet. I almost did once, after the prom with Charlie Freeber.

"I don't know." I shook my head. "She never tried to kiss me like I was a guy. I think Lottie's okay."

"You would," Violet said, and stepped away from the window.

***

My mom's family had eight brothers and sisters. My dad's had ten. I guess with that many kids in the family, there's bound to be some disagreements. My mom did not have a lot to say to her older brother, Uncle Sava, or his wife, Aunt Pamela. When Uncle Sava was a teenager, Baba thought he was getting seduced in his sleep by an evil spirit. Legend had it that our grandmother threw a knife into our uncle's bedroom door to keep the evil ghost woman away. By the time Violet and I were old enough to prowl around her house unattended, we'd found the gash in the attic door. And touched it.

"How could a knife in the door keep out evil spirits?" we three cousins wondered, when first acquiring this tantalizing bit of family history at Baba's house one summer.

We figured there must've been something on the knife. Or maybe Baba knew some magic. Self-consciously, I'd hidden my arm behind my back when we talked about the magical part, remembering what my grandmother had said about the trick she and I shared when I was a kid.

Mom and Uncle Sava had argued off and on since they were youngsters. Forced to move back home to conserve for the war effort, Mom and my sister, Hyacinth, and Uncle Sava's wife, Aunt Pamela, and her son, Cousin Milan, had been hard at it after Dad got home from World War Two and had to take Valiums for stress and high blood pressure. Mom said Uncle Sava could jump in the lake any time and it would be all right with her. She wondered who he thought he was: The King of France? Mom said Uncle Sava was arrogant and evil. When she said the evil part, Violet and I wondered if that bad ghost woman didn't get him in his sleep after all.

"Tell us the story about Grandpa's Daddy getting his head chopped off for sleeping with the farmer's wife," Boo said, snuggled into the blankets on the floor with me and Violet, since Aunt Lottie and her girlfriend had carted off the upstairs beds in their trailer. "Tell us the whole story, Ma, not just a little piece of it."

"Yeah," Violet and I said. We were ready for some family secrets.

"Oh, you girls," Aunt Sophie said, stretched out on the couch under her own blanket. "There's not much to tell."

By the time everyone left, half of the work was done on Baba's house, and all but Aunt Sophie were scheduled to stay overnight. (Uncle Tony and the boys had driven home to Detroit, but would be back in the early afternoon after a quick nine holes of golf.) When Boo and my twin and I found this out, we begged to stay overnight too. Mom brought back enough bedding and pajamas for us girls, as Cousin Boo was just about the same size as me and Violet. It was a slumber party campout. We jiggled around under the blankets, getting ready for a story, a real story without other adults around to censor out all the good parts.

"Come on," we three cousins begged.

Aunt Sophie got up and drew the living room shades against the night. She checked the doors. Boo and Violet and I looked at each other. We tucked the blankets under ourselves. This was going to be good.

"Well, let me see," Aunt Sophie said, settling back into her blankets. "I don't know that much about it." "Ma!" Boo complained.

"Calm down," Aunt Sophie said, "I'm thinking."

"You twins know your mother is going to be cross with me for filling your heads with all this nonsense."

"We won't tell," Violet said.

"Yeah," I said, "we won't tell."

"From what I understand, Grandpa Jeda's father, lived in a small village back in Serbia. He was an older man, married to a younger woman. You know, back in the Old Country, girls married very young. Sometimes they were only sixteen years old. I think Baba was only seventeen herself when she married Grandpa Jeda."

"That's young," Boo said. "That's only tenth grade."

"I don't think very many people went that far in school back then," Aunt Sophie said.

"So who cares?" Violet said.

"Okay, so, Grandpa's father was older and had lived alone for many years before he met his young wife, who would have been my Baba except she died in childbirth from having Jeda," Aunt Sophie said. "Many women did," she said, studying something on the ceiling.

"So when did Jeda's dad get his cabesa cut off?" Violet wanted to know.

"Sush!" Boo said.

"Hold on, I'm thinking," Aunt Sophie said. "So Grandpa Jeda and his father had a small farm. Everyone did. They used horses to plow their fields. They grew their own vegetables and other crops. Raised a few sheep. The two of them lived alone. I guess Jeda's father was quite the lady's man. They say he was very handsome. And he was a big man like Grandpa Jeda, and strong. When the blacksmith who took care of Grandpa's father's horse, caught Grandpa's father with his wife in the barn, he went after him. I guess they fought and grabbed whatever they could to hit each other with, and the blacksmith grabbed a heavy mallet that he used to hammer the horseshoes and hit grandpa in the head and knocked him out. They say he was so angry he got a sword and cut off Jeda's father's head. He would have done the same to his wife,

but she ran out of the barn before he could catch her."

"Wow," I said.

"Geez-o-Pete," Boo said.

"Cool," Violet said.

"So what did they do with his head?" Violet asked. "Or his body? Where did his wife run off to?"

"Getting your head cut off is awful." Boo made a face.

"How creepy," I said, and shuddered thinking about Grandpa's father's head rolling around on the ground.

"I don't know what they did with his head," Aunt Sophie said, "but I imagine the wife got stoned to death once they caught her."

"Stoned to death?" Boo made a scrunchy-face. She scooted around under the covers.

"With real stones?" I said, lost under imaginary floating heads.

"No, pretend ones, *estupida*," Violet said.

"Violet Jane," Aunt Sophie admonished. "Be nice."

"Well, what kind of a question is that? Real stones?" Violet said.

"I meant, how big?" I said. "Little pebbles or big rocks?"

"I imagine they were big enough to kill her," Aunt Sophie said.

"Kill her?" Boo's eyes just about disappeared in her face and she scooted around some more, pulling up the blankets, exposing our feet.

"Boo, stop messing up the covers," Violet said. "The bugs'll get at our feet."

"What bugs?" Boo asked.

"There aren't any bugs," Aunt Sophie said.

I hated bugs.

"Are there bugs down here, Ma?" Boo really wanted to know.

"There aren't any bugs," Aunt Sophie said, again. "Settle down."

"Well, what if there are?" I asked.

"Would you guys stop with the bugs, already?" Violet said. "I want to know what happened to the wife Grandpa Jeda's father was screwing."

Aunt Sophie looked at my sister.

"I don't know what happened to her," she said, "but I'm guessing she was stoned since the Ottoman Empire still ruled that part of the world, and they were Muslims. That's what they do with infidelity."

"With high-fidelity?" Boo asked.

"Infidelity," Violet informed her. "Geez,"

"What's *in* fidelity?" Boo asked.

"It's when husbands and wives sleep with people they're not married to," Violet said.

"Sleep?" Boo wondered.

"Have sex," Aunt Sophie seemed forced to say.

"Oh," Boo said.

"What was that?" Violet asked, out loud.

"What now?" Aunt Sophie said, in a tired voice.

"I thought I heard something in the kitchen," Violet said.

"You're being silly. It's all this talk of violence and the Old Country," Aunt Sophie said.

"There's nothing in the kitchen."

Violet said, "There it goes again."

Aunt Sophie said, "Shhhh!" like she meant it.

When something flapped over our heads, we all got crazy, hollering. We stood up in our places and jumped up and down, draping blankets over our heads like tents. Even Aunt Sophie hollered. She drew Boo to herself on the couch. She called Violet and me to join them and the five of us huddled together in our blankets, all wound up.

"What was that?" Everyone said.

"Shhh! Be still," Aunt Sophie warned. And we tried to be still until the flapping started all over again and ended up on top of my head.

"Ahh!" I hollered. "Get it off! Get if off!"

I carried on shaking the blanket over my head. I stood up on the couch.

"Help! Help!"

I leaped off the couch and ran around in a circle.

Suddenly we were all off the couch, shaking our blankets and dancing around like we had ants in our pants. When someone started running like we were Superman with our blankets flying behind us like a cape, we all did it.

"Ahh! Ahh!"

We went on in a circle.

"Get it off! Get it off!" we hollered, Aunt Sophie included.

"It's a bat! It's a bat!" Violet yelled out.

"It'll get in my hair!" Boo cried out. "Ma! Ma!"

"Help! Help!" I called out, doing the running thing and getting worn out so I stopped in my tracks, breathing hard, using my cape as a tent again.

Everyone else stopped being Superman and went back under their cape-tents, too. Now what?

"For pity's-sake!" Aunt Sophie sounded out of breath. "We're probably scaring the poor thing to death."

"But what if it bites?" Violet said. "They carry rabies."

"What if we get lock jaw and can't eat or talk and have to go to the hospital and get a bunch of shots?" I said, very concerned about the shots thing and starting to sweat.

"Don't you dare faint on us, Lilly June," Violet threatened, peeking out from under her blanket.

"Let's settle down and see if we can't catch it and put it outside," Aunt Sophie reconnoitered.

We wore our blankets like big babushkas and peeked around for the thing we guessed was a bat. When Aunt Sophie turned on the lights, a small black creature took a few laps over our heads before landing on a wall sconce.

"What the hell is that?" Violet said, without thinking there was an adult in the room.

"Looks like a bird with something in its mouth," Aunt Sophie squinted. "Violet Jane, does your mother know about your swearing?"

"I didn't swear," Violet said.

"Yes, you did," Boo said, looking at her from under her babushka blanket.

I didn't say anything as I wondered why anyone would care about swearing when there was a rabies-infected flying monster bird-bat on the loose in the house only inches away from our necks, ready to drink our blood before filling us with lock jaw for which we were probably going to get twelve shots in a circle in our stomachs. What if it was radioactive from the Nuclear Power Facility on Lake Erie? What if we were already contaminated and would sprout another arm or turn green and glow in the dark? What if...

"What's that in its mouth?" Aunt Sophie stepped closer. "Looks like a cicada."

"What's a cicada?" Boo asked.

"It's a bug," Violet said. "A big fly-looking bug."

"A bug!" Boo scrunched around under her blanket. "Ma!"

"Let's get something to catch it in and put it out," Aunt Sophie said.

"What's a bird doing en la casa?" Violet wondered aloud. "And how come it's flying around at night? I thought they did all their hunting in the day time."

"Well, maybe it got confused," Aunt Sophie said. "Come on."

We three kids stayed put. We were not going anywhere.

"Oh, all right, "sit back down on the couch and I'll find something," she said, struggling out of her blanket. "Stay out of the way then. Just a little bird. Probably more scared of us than we are of it."

I thought about how adults always said this about rabid wild animals. I thought about this from the safety of the couch under my tent-blanket-babushka.

"I thought birds in the house were no muy bueno," Violet said.

"I thought Baba said it meant we'd have company," I said.

"Maybe it just got lost, like Mom said," Boo said. "Ma, are birds in the house bad luck? Do they mean we'll have company?"

"I don't know." Aunt Sophie had returned with a broom and a pillowcase and was intent upon capturing the evil bird-bat with the nuclear bug in its beak. "I think it's just confused," she said, reaching with her broom.

"In the middle of the night?" Violet said, from her couch tent. "I read in The National Enquirer once where some birds only fly around at night and end up attacking people like they're vampire bats, but it's someplace in South America like Uruguay. Some kind of a disease messes up their brains and they end up acting like bats. Flying around at night and shit, I mean stuff. There might be a couple that migrated to New York City along with the tarantulas on banana boats," she said with authority.

"Isn't it too cold?" I wondered. I must've said out loud that I thought the *National Enquirer* was not an encyclopedia because Violet said, "At least I read. You never read anything."

"I don't like to read," I said. Truth was, I got laughed at in first grade by everyone in my reading circle when the word coming out of my mouth was not the same as the written word on the page where everybody else was pointing their fingers. I tried about five or six times before I got it right but by then, tears had pooled in my eyes and I decided reading was verboten. When you got into second grade you were expected to sound out all the words in your head, silently and by yourself. Watching TV was not painful or lonely. I didn't have to say the words to myself in my head or figure out anything. And there could be other people around too.

"I can't help it if you got a reading problem," Violet said. "*The National Enquirer* said they might hibernate in caves."

"Tarantulas don't hibernate, do they, Ma?" Boo asked.

"What are you and the twins talking about now?"

Aunt Sophie took a swing at the vampire bird with the mutant bug. It careened over our tented heads before cornering itself in the vestibule. Aunt Sophie covered her head with the pillowcase and opened the door to the outside world where the night sucked up the winged animal in its maw.

We all clapped.

Boo jumped off the couch to hug her mother.

"Ma, what's a bird doing in the house at night?" she asked.

"I don't know," Aunt Sophie replied, settling down on the couch and scooting me and my sister off. "You and the twins can go back to the floor now that the poor bird is gone. I think we've had enough excitement for one night."

Boo, Violet and I settled into our pallets on the floor in front of the couch. We organized our blankets. We fiddled around trying to find the best spot.

"I have to go to the bathroom," Cousin Boo announced.

"Me too," I added, crawling out from my blanket.

"Ma," Boo said, "I'm scared. What if there's another wild bird in the house or one of those migrating tarantulas that didn't hibernate?"

"There aren't any other animals in the house." Aunt Sophie sounded exhausted.

"But what if?" Boo asked.

"You two better get going," she said.

On the stairway, I heard my aunt tell Violet to keep the stories in *The National Enquirer* to herself and that she was glad my sister read but that some magazines were more suitable reading material than others. I heard Violet say she also read *National Geographic*. My twin was a real patriot as she only read materials with the word National in the title.

Boo and I turned on the light at the bottom of the stairway. Together, we synchronized our feet on each step watching for birds that thought they were vampire bats and giant spiders that did not hibernate. Eventually, and with great care, we made it to the top of the stairs. We took two steps to the left. From our vantage point, we could either turn left again and go to the bathroom, or turn right and see directly into Grandpa Jeda's bedroom and out through the window that looked across the lot to the next-door neighbor's house. The moon lit up the night in a shiny darkness, acting like a flashlight in Jimmie Connor's upstairs window where he stood in what looked like a pair of pink long johns with a slinky attached to his crotch. Boo and I looked at each other and tiptoed into Jeda's bedroom, nearly touching our noses to the window pane.

"He's bare-naked," Boo whispered.

"What's that?" I whispered.

"Looks like he's standing in the window bare-naked," Boo repeated as if this clarified things.

"But what's that?" I whispered again, my finger on the window.

"It's his thing," Boo whispered.

As if Jimmie Connor heard us, he grabbed his slinky and wiggled it, crazy grin on his face. He jumped up and down a couple of times before turning around and pressing his rear-end against the windowpane. Boo and I looked at each other and turned around, running past St. John the Baptist keeping watch from the wall, as Aunt Lottie and her girlfriend must've left him behind when they took the bed. Cousin Boo and I hurried through our business in the bathroom and rushed downstairs like we were holding our breath. We turned out the light and jumped under our covers.

Violet and Aunt Sophie were already asleep in their blankets.

"Why was Jimmie Connor standing in the window bare-naked?" Boo wanted to know.

"I don't know," I whispered, organizing myself under my blanket, making sure nothing was sticking out.

"Do you think he saw us?" Boo whispered back.

"I think he must've. I think he wanted us to see him."

"Why would he want us to see him bare-naked?" Boo wondered.

"Once, when Violet and me were little, Mike Houser, from down the block, used to stand in the window without any clothes on our way to school in the morning. He'd knock on the window for us to look up. At first, it was only me who saw him, but then Violet and Barb Pagroti saw him, too. When Violet and Barb and I told Mom, she said it was hard to believe since Mike Houser came from a good family, but we didn't walk to school that way anymore."

"I never saw anyone's thing before," I said.

"I saw my brothers' before," Boo said. "They're funny looking. Do you think we should tell my ma?"

"I don't know," I said. "Sure was creepy the way he made a face. Looked like a crazy man."

"Yeah," Boo agreed, scooching under her blanket. "What about Violet? Should we tell her?"

"She'll make a big deal about it and tell us some story out of *The National Enquirer*."

Both Boo and I laughed. We decided that there was something wrong with Jimmie Connor, and that we'd tell Aunt Sophie about the whole thing in the morning.

I don't know what Boo thought about before falling asleep, but my head was jammed up with rabid birds turning into vampires with mutant bugs in their mouths, bare-naked neighbor boys with slinkies in their pants, St. John the Baptist still hanging out in Grandpa's bedroom, Crazy Julia rolling cigarettes and catching schizophrenia from her appendix operation, Aunt Lottie kissing her movie star girlfriend, Jeda's dad getting his head chopped off and the blacksmith's wife getting beat to death with rocks, Baba stabbing Uncle Sava's bedroom door with a knife to keep away the evil ghost woman seducer, the other ghost who laid on top of old Mrs. Wozjec, and Cousin Debbie losing her mind to the Harry Criscos.

After a while, I forgot about the crazy stuff and found myself outside in the darkness, high in the sky on the back of a giant bird. The same one I dreamed of when I was a kid. Huge, brown eagle's wings outstretched. Baba was with me this time too, only she wasn't old anymore; she was the same age as me. She wore only an apron, like she did when she used to go swimming in the Old Country. The girl Baba was blue-eyed beautiful, long blond braids ribboned across her bare back, and she sat behind me on the winged horse huge bird as we sliced through the air happy in our flight. Just the two of us on the grand magical creature. The air both warm and cool against our skin. We laughed at ourselves as we rose and fell with the great animal in the black light. No one spoke except the giant phoenix who uttered a single word.

I strained to hear him.

He spoke again, but the wind took his word away.

"What?" I said. "Please?"

Baba put her hand over my mouth and whispered "Shhhh" into my ear.

"But what did he say?" I said.

"Shhhh," Baba said again, "you'll wake the others."

"Huh?" I said, and with great effort, forced my eyes open.

Confused into reality, I found myself blinking on the floor by the vestibule, away from everyone else. I remembered the great bird and the beautiful girl Baba riding behind me. The feel of the night. Then I remembered Baba telling me to shhhh or I'd wake the others. Weird. Dream time and real time crisscrossing. I crawled over to where Cousin Boo and Violet Jane lay sleeping on the floor and got back under my covers. Thought itchy, I jumped up and went into the kitchen for a glass of water, looking out the window as I filled the glass from the cold water faucet.

Outside, the night was moon-bright still. Shadows cut across the lawn in sharp geometric designs. The ground was shiny silver fairytales. I took slow, cool swallows, imagining things in the night. I closed my eyes against the window theater and revisited the great bird of my dreams and the girl Baba. For long moments, I stood silent in the kitchen, slowly drawing water into my mouth, breathing inside the glass, and re-riding my dream.

A clap from the basement brought me back. I put my glass in the sink and listened without breathing. When no other sound came, I crept to the edge of the stairway and leaned forward over the top of the first step, holding my breath. I listened again. Nothing.

Most everyone came back to work at Baba's house the next day. When Dad went down the basement to check the pilot light on the furnace, he discovered an open window. Aunt Sophie said it was probably how "the poor little bird found its way into the house," and "you girls running around probably didn't help," and "the poor helpless thing was probably scared half to death when it couldn't find its way out."

When I said I'd heard something in the basement after the incident with the bird, everybody thought it must have been the wind except Violet, who told me and Boo later that she thought it was Grandpa Jeda's ghost come back to lay on top of us, and Cousin Boo, who said she wondered if the evil ghost woman who seduced Uncle Sava had returned, and I, who wondered, but didn't say anything, about the dream girl Baba telling me to shhhh as she covered my mouth with her hand.

When Boo and I told our mothers about bare-naked Jimmie Connor from next-door with his hind-end mashed against the window, both our mothers said we probably imagined it since it was at night, and what were we doing looking in his window anyway? When Mom said he would never do such a silly thing as he came from a good family and all, I could see gears going around in her head about the good family part, even as she said it. Then Violet wanted to know why we didn't wake her up so she could see the "bare-naked guy with his ass in the window" too. I guess she felt she missed out on some priceless odd item and wouldn't be able to catalogue, first hand, the actual fact in her mental library of the weird and the weirder along with her clippings from *The National Enquirer*. She didn't see me smile about it either.

Chapter 9.

DEEPEES, GYPSIES, AND THE GERMAN WAR BRIDE

They were having a slava at Vucovich's farm on Bluebush Road. Violet and I hadn't been to one of these foreign feasts since we were kids, and we were sort of looking forward to it. We'd been raised Episcopalian all our lives and had been very Americanized. The only Serbian Orthodox Church in Custer, Michigan was across the tracks in the East End, and Mom would not attend except for Bingo. Of the other churches she'd had to choose from in town, she'd claimed St. John's Episcopal Church was the closest to the Serbian Orthodox Church. The Roman Catholics were close, too, and there were plenty of them, but we'd have had to climb over her dead body to go to one. Mom was a traditionalist in many ways. She held on to some kind of an historical schism that divided the Christians in Rome from the ones in Constantinople. The only real Christian churches were, of course, those churches emanating from the original orthodoxy in Constantinople before the Pope stuck his big nose into everything. We celebrated two Christmases and two Easters because of a calendar schism between these two seats. The whole thing became verboten, however, after Baba died. I guess Mom felt her crusade for the historical elders had gone on long enough.

Mom also held onto a few personal schisms of her own, like with Uncle Sava after World War Two and buying frozen dessert that wasn't Neapolitan ice milk.

"Isn't it against the law to call it ice cream when it's really frozen milk?" Violet asked, leaning on the freezer door. "We should call the

92

damn police or write our congressman about it. We never have anything good to eat in this house unless Dad goes to the store, and then he gets yelled at."

She took out the carton, closed the door and looked around.

"Who's in charge around here anyway? They go to Independent Dairy at Barb's house. They got fudge ripple and tin roof ice cream at Barb's house. Real ice cream. There's always something great to eat at Barb's house."

Violet opened the half-gallon carton she'd been holding in her hand.

"Christ. Look at this? We're stuck with this stupid glob of pink crap. Hell, Dad won't even eat it. Mom's the only one who likes this crap anyway, and she won't eat it when it gets all hard and crusty but then won't buy any more until this shit's gone. I hate this place."

Violet had her schisms, too

"You know they won't have ice milk at the slava. They'll probably have Good Humor Bars and Drumsticks and Pushups---good shit like that. Plus all the cakes and pastries the old grandmas make." Violet licked her lips. "And Hires Root beer and Orange Crush. Real stuff. Not store brand crapshit. Wonder who's gonna be there. Wonder if any of the cousins will be there."

"I like the roast lamb they turn on the spit in the hole they dig in the ground. It's the best," I said, almost tasting the garlic and salt. "How come stuff always tastes better outside and with a whole bunch of people around? Even hotdogs on a grill?"

"Probably because Mom didn't make it," Violet said. "Ever notice how she cooks like she's in a race? Everything boils over and gets scorched. Everything's brown or olive green." She made a face. "Our stove looks like a war zone."

"I notice the pots and pans after," I said.

As we turned in to park, I heard the Tambouritzan Orchestra singing and playing their Old Country songs on acoustic guitar and stand up bass, violin and mandolin. Cars were backed up along the dirt road and on the lawn when we arrived. Music blared from a microphone beyond the trees. Smoke rose high overhead and laughter charged the air. Images of being five years old played in my mind: running barefoot in the grass, spilling something on my dress, and crying over a skinned knee, but mostly, being allowed to play freely and unattended within our small rabble of cousins.

When we were little, Violet and I used to run in and out of the adults who stood in small groups or hopped up and down to the music. We chased each other across the grass, carried around soggy paper plates until their contents fell to the ground, drank colored pop, and got sick. We played Red Rover with the clasped hands of the adults as they danced and hollered. Mom was a good hollerer, and I hoped to acquire the same skill when I grew up. Everybody thought I was too darling when I belted out my puny five-year old screech, hopping up and down next to Mom.

The stada babas, in their wrapped braids and babushkas, stood in groups separate from their men folk who laughed and smoked their pipes behind their handlebar moustaches. Old Country Serbs stood arm in arm, singing and wiping their eyes and noses with their handkerchiefs. Every adult male carried a family handkerchief. Besides drying their tears brought on by songs from the homeland, they never knew if they were going to get hauled onto the dance floor to bring up the rear-end of a kolo, and you'd better be ready to flag the air with your hanky and holler and stomp and know what you're doing. Hanky holding was serious business.

I remember Mom seemed to let go of the reins and rules at these Serbian picnics. She danced, and hollered, and made requests of the Tambouritzan Orchestra. She spurdinesed (Serbian for teased) with people. She hugged and kissed our dad. She was warm and friendly like a TV mom, and we took advantage of it. When she sat down to catch her breath, Violet and I took turns sitting on her lap, feeling special. She continually rearranged herself against our bony butts, acting like we were thousand pound sacks squashing her boobs. To me, she felt like a pillow. To her, we must have felt like the mangler.

Dad used to have fun at the slavas, too, even if he was a Croat who'd been raised Roman Catholic. I figured Mom must've forgiven him these two crimes since he was so big and handsome. Dad was the hub in my emotional wheel. He was always a willing partner for Violet and me. It didn't matter if we were at a Serbian picnic, or fishing at Carter's Bay, or driving the Pink Swan, or hanging out in the TV room watching *Gunsmoke* or Sid Caesar and Imogene Coca, he was available. And happy about it.

"Me!" I reached for him with both my five year old arms. "Pick me up, Dad!"

I jumped up and down on my toes. He was smoking an R.G. Dunn and talking to a Romanian man newly arrived to The States who spoke in heavily accented English and easy Serbo-Croatian. He and Dad toasted their health with a shot of slivovitz. I understood pieces of their conversations, as Violet and I knew some of the old tongue. They talked about the iron ore range in Minnesota where my dad grew up. Mom said the Romanian man was a DeePee like it was a secret.

"Me, too, Dad!" Violet reached and jumped up and down next to me. "Me, too."

Dad laughed and extended both his hands to us: One to me and one to my twin sister. We each grabbed a huge paw with both hands. Dad smiled around the R.G Dunn that curled in his eyes, letting us steer him onto the dance floor.

"Okay," Dad said. "Okay, you two. Let me get rid of this cigar."

"I'll hold it." Violet reached over to him.

Dad tapped the burning ash.

"Be careful," he said as he handed it to her. "Maybe you two are too big for me to carry now that you're almost in kindergarten," he teased. "I don't know?"

"Daaad!" We both begged, pulling on him and jiggling around.

"Okay," he laughed. "Who's first?"

"Me! Me!" We stood on our toes reaching up. "Me! Me!"

In one movement, Dad put one arm around my waist and the other around my twin's. Together, he lifted us both in his arms. Violet wrapped one arm around Dad and held out his R. G. Dunn with the other like it was poison. I held on with both hands.

I remember the three of us danced around as one unit. We twirled and glided side-to-side, forward and backward. Dad sang and laughed. People smiled. Mom sang too and clapped along with the music. When we got over to Hyacinth, Dad asked if she'd take his cigar. She held it out from her like it was a dead animal in one hand

and drew on her Hires Root Beer bottle with the other. She stood with Cousins Debbie and Danitsa, and Second Cousins Eva and Dirk. Second Cousin Dirk tried to take Dad's R.G. Dunn away from her, but his mom, Cousin Elisa, cuffed him on the back of the head. Cousin Elisa was not a real cousin. She was married to one of Aunt Lottie's kids, Cousin Milo, who was as old as Mom and Dad. Cousin Milo was also in World War Two like my dad. Cousin Elisa was from Germany, and she and Cousin Milo got married and had Eva and Dirk the Jerk, who really wasn't a jerk, but Violet thought it rhymed. Mom said Cousin Milo's wife, Cousin Elisa, looked like an "air-e-an" with her pale blond hair and pointed nose. Mom said Cousin Elisa was a German war bride like it was something to be ashamed of.

Thoughts of times past floated around behind my eyes as I hurried from the car. I grew anxious for the roast lamb and mentally practiced Old Country dance steps in my head. Kids ran after each other, barefoot across the grass, toppling their soggy plates like Hansels and Gretels. The weather held, and the sun shone hard on the ground. Instead of happy party dresses, Violet and I wore shorts because at fourteen, neither of us would've been caught dead in a dress at a picnic---any picnic---slava or not. Our ma-toor-ing was grindingly slow, as we were still in training bras, though what we were training for was beyond me. Dresses were now stupid and shorts were cool. I wondered if there were any Good Humor bars left. Did someone think to make potica (that honey and walnut pastry)? I could only hope someone else's grandma could cook.

"Hey, Lilly! Hey, Violet!" Cousin Boo waved, skipping up to us in a pair of plaid Bermuda shorts.

"Hey!" I called back, smiling hard.

"Hey, yourself," said Violet. "Cool pants."

"Oh, these?" Boo looked down, "Yeah, I got them yesterday at Hudson's. I bought them myself with money I got for my birthday."

"Mom didn't know if you were coming or not," I said, looking at my cousin but keeping an ear to the music.

"Bobby drove. Dad's at a golf tournament," Boo said. "Mom said Bobby could drive here and she could drive home. He didn't want to come, but he wanted to drive, so he's in a crabby mood.

The only thing is we got to leave before it gets dark since Mom hates to drive in the dark."

"Bobby got to drive, huh?" Violet said.

"Yeah," Boo said.

"How old is he?" Violet asked.

"Sixteen his last birthday," Boo answered.

"So where is everybody?" Violet asked.

Boo turned and pointed to the dance platform and barbeque drums as pits were no longer used. She walked with Violet and me and Mom and Dad, and Hyacinth toward the music and partygoers. My heart beat faster, watching the parade of happy people. Lightness of spirit lifted me, and the world seemed good. Look at all this! I thought to myself, and laughed out loud. I felt Violet's sneer and didn't care. When Boo asked me what was so funny, I told her everything was so funny. We grinned at each other and trotted over to where it was all going on.

Dad bought a reel of tickets and allowed Violet and me to buy whatever we wanted. I loaded up with roast lamb and Serbian pastries. No green pop for me this time as I'd acquired a taste for Vernors, what with all the migraines and stuff. And I wasn't taking any chances on throwing up at fourteen and in front of everyone. Violet went for ice cream first, as she wasn't taking any chances on getting ice milk. Both of us were free, and we were going for it. No broiling pots and pans and mashed canned peas. No beige and brown glop. No sour green apple pies for us.

After easily working my way through a delectable mound of tasty treats before my paper plate had a chance to wilt and dump its contents on the ground, Boo and I ran up to the wooden platform and hopped up and down with the rest of them for all we were worth. Sometimes Boo caught the end of a circle kolo and got to wave her hanky. When it was me at the end, I hollered and waved like I was my mom.

"Where's Violet Jane?" Boo wanted to know, after we plopped down on folding chairs to get a breath.

"Don't know. And don't want to know," I told her.

She looked at me.

"You two don't do everything together? I thought twins did everything together?"

"Sometimes she goes to Barb's house without me and other stuff," I said. "We don't have to be together all the time. Plus, she thinks I need to find my own friends and stop bugging her. She says I'm a royal pain."

"I thought you and Violet had the same friends?"

"We do," I said, looking out at the people in front of us having a great time.

Hyacinth and Cousin Danitsa were shuffling and gliding across the dance floor, doing extra fancy steps they'd learned at Saturday Serbian School at St. George's Eastern Orthodox Church. Dad had a cigar in his hand, and Mom had her arms around another woman as they sang and cried with the Tambouritzans.

"How can you find your own friends if you've got the same ones?" Boo asked.

"I guess we have to visit them at different times," I said. "I haven't figured it out yet."

"Violet's not very nice," Boo said.

"I don't want to talk about Violet. Right now I'm making my own friends," I said, smiling at Cousin Boo.

"Yeah," she said, laughing back. "Let's go get something to eat."

Like little kids, we ran off to the pastry table where we found Aunt Sophie making a plate for Boo's little brother, Ronnie, and herself.

"There you are," Aunt Sophie said to Boo and gave her a warm smile. "Lilly June, I saw you up there dancing. You've got a voice like your ma."

I grinned.

"Where's Violet?" she asked.

"They can have their own friends, Ma," Boo said. "They don't have to do everything together." Boo looked at me and smiled.

"I haven't seen her," I said.

"Grace, would you mind going to the car and getting me my cigarettes? I thought I had some in my purse, but I can't find them.

Must have left them in the glove box. Would you go check for me, honey?"

"Sure," Boo answered, and we took off on a run.

"Shhh," Boo had her finger to her mouth as their car came into view. She pulled me down to a crouch. We reconnoitered under a tree.

"Look who's in the front seat with Bobby," she whispered.

It was Violet. She and Bobby had their arms hanging outside either side of the front seat windows. They were slouched down, their heads leaning against the headrests. They looked to be smoking Aunt Sophie's cigarettes.

"Let's sneak up on them and see what they're doing," Boo said.

"I think the Mo-town sound is really bitchin'," Violet said around her cigarette. She flicked an ash out the window like she'd been doing it all her life. "Smoky and the Temps are the most."

Cousin Bobby let out a plume of smoke, "Yeah, Marvin Gaye's really got the sound, man."

He sang a few bars about hearing it through the grapevine. Then he got to tapping out the rhythm on the steering wheel with the cigarette hanging out of his mouth like he was forty years old.

Boo and I had to pinch ourselves to keep from laughing. Through hand signs, we decided we'd each take a window. We got ready. On the count of three we stood up and yelled,"Gotcha!"

Violet choked on a pull of smoke and coughed until I thought her eyes were going to fall out. Bobby dropped his cigarette in his lap and butt-hopped around in his seat, trying to brush the ashes from his pants. Swear words like wet hornets careened around inside the car. Boo yelled that her ma wanted her cigarettes, and she was going to tell. Bobby threw open the car door and took off after her. I stayed back and laughed at Violet.

"Damn it, Lil. Grow up!" Violet wheezed, stubbing out her cigarette.

"Grow up yourself," I told her under my breath, and walked away into the crowd of happy party people, reflexively hunching my shoulders against a possible pounding on the back.

A heavyset woman wearing a long black dress and wild hair

crossed in front of me. Silver and gold bangles jangled on her wrists. She wore rings on every finger and carried a red plastic cup in each hand. Cinnamon and cloves followed her as she passed by. I watched her float into a group of dark-skinned people. She stopped when she got to the DP from Romania that I remembered from when I was a kid. The small knot of like kind wore dark clothes and dark hair. One man had a ponytail. She and the DP touched cups and bolted down their drinks. When he leaned into her, she threw her head back and laughed deeply, combing her ringed fingers through her unruly hair. She was exotic and mesmerizing, and I stood, transfixed. When she brought her head down, she turned her dark eyes to me and nodded. Without thinking, I nodded back. We locked eyes for a moment, and then she turned away.

"Boy is Bobby in trouble." Boo ran up behind me breathing hard. "What are you looking at?"

"What?" I said, lost behind my eyes.

"What are you looking at?" Boo repeated, following the direction of my stare. "Those DP's?" she said. "Ma said they're gypsies. She said they're from Romania. She said they go to St. George's."

"Huh?" I said.

"Do you think we can get them to read our palms or tell our fortunes?" Boo asked. "Wouldn't it be cool?"

"Maybe," I said, clearing my head. "Maybe I don't want to know what's coming up."

"Like maybe they'd tell us when we were gonna die or something."

"Yeah, maybe."

"Maybe they could tell us about Grandpa Jeda's ghost laying on top of everybody," Boo said. "Or what birds in the house mean at night like when we all slept over at Baba's. That was pretty spooky until Ma got it out. Do you think it was a radioactive bat, like what Violet said?"

Boo laughed.

"Remember Jimmie Connor with his bare-naked butt in the window? When I told Bobby, he said that Jimmie was shooting the moon."

"That was something," I said, hearing my cousin only sort of.

"Lilly," Boo said. "Lilly!"

"Yeah."

"Get with it." Boo shook my arm. "You act like you're in a trance or something."

I blinked and shook my head.

"Let's go find Violet." I shivered. "See if she's got extra tickets. I'm hungry."

"I got some." Boo pulled out a length from her pocket.

"Let's see how much Violet's got left," I insisted, wanting to see my twin sister.

We found her sulking next to Mom and Aunt Sophie who were holding soggy paper plates. She slouched in a folding chair with her arms crossed, legs stretched out in front. When she saw Boo and me approaching, she stuck out her tongue.

"There you girls are," Mom said to me and Boo. "Where have you two been? Have you eaten anything?"

"We came for more tickets," Boo said, holding up her strip.

"I have a few left," Mom said, giving hers to me. "Go find your father."

She turned to Violet.

"Why don't you join Grace and your sister? See if you can stay out of trouble."

Reluctantly, Violet pushed herself out of her chair. And the three of us meandered through the rowdy clutches of people until we found Dad, who gave us plenty of money for tickets. Then we ate until we got sick, just like in the good old days.

On the way home, Dad puffed on his cigar. And just like in the good old days, I turned green in the back seat. Carsick since I was a little kid, I'd been allowed access to a window that I was permitted to crack open even in the winter. Mom still kept a shoebox and hand towel on the floor of the backseat for me. Up until a couple of years ago, I used to stare out the car window, trying to focus on a pebble in the pavement. I'd look straight down to the road beneath as we rushed by at fifty miles an hour. Only took a mile or so of this nonsense, and I was cross-eyed and puking in the shoebox. Add a little cigar smoke, and I'd had it. I don't know how I missed the part of car passenger etiquette where I was supposed to look up and out the window, over the landscape, enjoying the view, evaluating buildings and barns, homes and outside décor. I must have been in one of my altered states during that teensy weensy vehicular lesson.

Nobody else in the car figured out what I was doing, either, until Mom said something about a cow in a field. We'd been packed into the Blue Goose (the Pink Swan had been traded up), doing our yearly trek to Minnesota to see Dad's family. There must have been a breakthrough in my Dramamine-induced coma because I was actually able to respond to brief commands. I wiped the drool from my mouth and opened my eyes. And I saw a cow. In a field. I blinked. I rubbed my eyes. I sat up. There she was in all her glory. The kind of black and white Daisy cow I'd seen a hundred times on TV. A single cow. Just an ordinary everyday cow she was. And she was beautiful! She was brilliant. Wow and well, well. There it is, boys and girls. I'd made it into the secret club of happy car riders. I sat up straighter. I enjoyed the view. Why, I even participated in conversations with my family. And on occasion, I, myself, pointed out things on the horizon for others to see. Unless, of course, Dad lit up one of his stogies, hurtling me into a dark well of greasy queasiness.

Because it was still warm out, we rode home from the slava with the windows open. I kept my nose in the open air and thought about the day. After a while, I pulled myself up to Mom in the front seat.

"Mom, who was that lady with all the bracelets and rings talking to the DP?"

She looked to Dad to clear up what I meant.

He said, "That's Kosko, the Romanian guy who's got family in Minnesota."

"Oh, you mean Sosha Bennish," Mom said. "She and Rudy go to St. George's. They've got a couple of girls Hyacinth's age. Didn't you see them? They're very talented dancers."

"I saw a bunch of people who looked like them," I said. "One guy had a ponytail."

"I think he's a nephew. I understand he's recently arrived."

"They dress different," I said, before sitting back to stick my nose out the window.

"Yeah, I know who you mean." Violet sat up. "They look like gypsies. The *National Geographic* says that gypsies originated from India and that they don't need passports to go from one country to the next. And that they can't really tell fortunes and crap, I mean stuff. I read in The National Enquirer, though, that they live in caravans and have crystal balls and can read palms and predict the future with special cards called tear-outs. Some of them might even be vampires." Violet sat back. "Geez, we should've had them read our palms."

"Violet Jane, wherever do you get this nonsense? I have told you before that some material is not fit to read. Just because it's in print does not make it so. Why can't you read Nancy Drew or Clara Barton? Something suitable for girls your age. Honestly."

Mom turned around.

"Don't you dare ask Mr. or Mrs. Bennish to read your palms."

She turned back.

"And they do not live in caravans." She looked at Dad. "They live a couple of blocks over on West Willow."

"No shoot?" Violet said. "Cool."

"So, are they gypsies?" I asked, sitting up.

"There aren't any more tsegongas. Mr. and Mrs. Bennish are just colorful people," Mom said. "He works at Consolidated with your father, and she works at the East End bakery where we get those fresh loaves of bread on Friday night."

"Really?" I said, "I've never seen her there before."

"Well, she does."

"Wow, a real gypsy woman," I said.

"Don't call them gypsies," Mom said, like it she meant it.

"Is she a DP like the Romanian guy Dad was talking to?" I asked.

"I don't know," Mom said. "I don't think so."

"So who gets to be a Romanian guy and who gets to be a gypsy?" I was confused.

"What are you talking about?"

"Are DP's and gypsies the same thing?" I asked.

"They could be," Mom said, which didn't help me out much.

"How can they be?" I was mixed up.

"DP stands for Displaced Persons," Mom said. "It's an abbreviation."

"So it's D period, P period," I said.

"Uh huh."

"So what's a Displaced Person?" Violet asked, sitting up behind Dad, her hands on his backrest.

"He could be anyone who has lost his country," Mom said.

"How can you lose your country?" Violet asked. "Can't just disappear into thin air. Poof. *Finito.*"

"A person could be driven out by war or persecution. Sometimes the government confiscates landholdings," Mom said. "The Ottoman Turks took land away from the Yugoslavs. The Germans took land away from the Jews."

I thought about this and felt bad for the D.P.'s and the Yugoslavs and the Jews. I sat back and put my nose to the open window. I breathed deep. I had thought D.P's had done something bad, and here, it turns out that someone had done something bad to the D.P.'s. Suddenly I wanted to apologize to the Romanians and the D.P.'s, the gypsies and the Jews.

Violet and I both sat back, quiet during the rest of the ride home. I kept my nose to the open window, and Violet did the same. Dad put out his cigar and turned on the radio. Mom leaned over and gave him a kiss. Silent through our conversation about D.P's and gypsies, Hyacinth Suzanne put her hand on my knee. She looked at Violet. An old people's radio station played through the green dayglo dials. The instrumental music was soothing and inviting. It encapsulated our little family as we motored in and out under the streetlights. We had a country. We had a home. And right now, we had each other.

Chapter 10.

SECOND COUSIN EVA POOPED IN THE BACKYARD

When we were eight years old, Second Cousin Eva pooped in our backyard. She left a turd the size of a small boa constrictor next to the back porch steps---the biggest turd I ever saw, wrapped around like links of kielbasa. She told us not to watch her do it, but like that was not going to happen. When we saw her at an ethnic picnic, years later.

Violet asked her, "So Second Cousin Eva, what's with the pile of shit you left in our backyard back when we were kids?"

Second Cousin Eva got red in the face and said, "Mother told me I couldn't use the bathroom."

Violet said, "What the hell?"

I said, "What the hell?" too, feeling it was worth the risk.

Chapter 11.

HIDDEN TALENTS

I used to play the cello. I wasn't very good at it, but I liked the sound it made when I drew my bow across the strings. I gave it up for two reasons. One reason was that I couldn't get my left hand to quiver over the wires, no matter how many times Miss Anderson showed me in sixth hour music practice. And it started to feel like the first grade reading problem. Violet played the violin. We were both in orchestra from fifth through most of eighth grade. I don't think my twin got the hang of the quivering left hand thing, either. In the meantime, Mom bought a piano: A stand up in the corner kind. It was a Steinway.

"What's with the piano?"

Violet and I had been sitting on the stairway, watching two sweaty guys with butt cracks grunt over the heavy instrument.

"I want my girls to learn to play the piano," she replied, smiling to herself as she caressed the keys.

"I'm not gonna play that thing!" Violet said. "Gosh darn it all!"

"Watch your language," Mom said absently, a faraway look in her eyes.

"Well, geez-o-petes," Violet whined. "I'm still playing the violin!"

Mom hummed to herself as she wiped her palm over the top of her piano.

"I'm not very musical," I added, wondering how I was going to manage the cello and the piano, since I wasn't very good at what I already played.

"You can either play both instruments or give up the cello and violin," Mom said lightly, already falling in love with her Steinway.

"Crap," Violet said under her breath as she turned around and stomped upstairs.

She'd have slammed her bedroom door if she'd have had one to slam.

The parents, Hyacinth, and I all had doors to our bedrooms. Violet's room was a combination sewing room and parlor. It had an open archway. My twin must've been visiting one of her girlfriends when she and I got to call our rooms. I think I had the best one. Three windows, a closet, and bathroom around the corner. The only bad part was old man Krepps and I could see each other if we both looked out our bedroom windows at the same time. I usually kept my shade halfway open, unless I was changing my clothes.

As it turned out, Violet and I gave up our stringed instruments and dropped out of the Custer Junior High orchestra. The second reason I gave up the cello was because it was a rental, and I didn't have any money of my own to pay for it, and Mom wasn't going to spend her hard earned money on it and the piano. My sister's violin was already paid for. Violet stubbornly practiced her violin in the early evenings after dinner, screeching along, merrily working at the quivering left hand thing. Both of us got commandeered into piano lessons anyway, no matter. We hated it. And we got regular report cards in piano, too. Neither one of us practiced, so I was surprised when my grades improved. I played boogie- woogie, and my sister played classical. She played Fur Elise until the cows came home. I played it too, when her music book was left out. Normally, she kept her books hidden.

During the lessons, I liked the sound of the piano and even thought I'd pick it up until I got home and realized I wasn't cut out for piano, even though no quivering left hand was necessary. I don't think Violet was that good at it either. We played regardless because Mom wanted us to, and she was paying for it. I think she thought it would give us culture. We couldn't practice if Dad was home, though. He had only one good ear on him since World War Two, but that one ear was tuned to high-pitched sounds. He thought someone was talking to him whenever we practiced. He kept calling "What?" and "Damnit!" all the time until Mom caught on.

Hyacinth did not escape the piano thing, either, but she got to keep her clarinet since the folks already paid for it. She got to stay in the Custer High School band. And it was while she was at band camp that we moved from our house on Godfrey Street to the one on Elm Avenue. I guess it slipped the parents' mind to tell Hyacinth Suzanne before they dropped her off at school for the waiting bus, that we were moving while she was at camp. It was arranged with my sister's friend, Margorie Bouchard, to give her a ride home when they returned after the week at camp. I heard that Hyacinth waited around in the dark on the front porch steps of our old locked up house, holding her clothes bag and clarinet until one of the neighbors saw her and told her we'd moved. She ended up dragging her things to Aunt Amelia's house who told her we'd moved and where to and how to get there. I wondered for a long time if there was any permanent psychological damage to my older sister because of it.

When I was in second grade, I won a coloring contest by coloring Zippy the Monkey in a special section of the Custer Daily Newspaper. I used crayons and stayed in the lines. I won a brand new blue bicycle. Violet got an honorable mention and was invited to the cake and ice cream party with Zippy and me. Zippy got cake and ice cream in his hair and on my dress. He smelled and wore a diaper in his pants. I won ribbons and trophies in 4-H Club, Girl Scouts of America, Riverside Elementary School, Christiancy Middle School and Custer Junior High School, but I thought Frankie Banyon was a better artist. He did too.

I had other talents, but none of them involved reading. I hated to read since I was in first grade and figured I was doing okay without Nancy Drew and the Hardy Boys. My twin sister was a really good reader. Once she read *Ivanhoe* in the car all the way to Minnesota until Mom discovered it was *Peyton Place*. In fourth grade, Mrs. Wells read *The Little House on the Prairie* books to us after recess. I could have listened to her read forever. We gutted through *Silas Marner* in Miss Greenwald's seventh grade English last year. We read sections out loud. Even I read my part without stuttering and passing out. Miss Greenwad, as Violet used to call her, booger breath if my sister was feeling particularly clever, said we could expect more of the same kind of "wonderful classics" we experienced in *Silas Marner* as we got older. I never knew who or what *Silas Marner* was. I think it was supposed to be a poem, but it didn't rhyme and was way too long. It was a story about a guy named Silas Marner, but that's about all I got out of it. Miss Greenwald walked around on tiptoes in her taffeta dresses like a librarian when we had quiet time reading in our seats. Her breath smelled like throw-up, which discouraged me from asking questions. I stayed confused about Mr. Marner. English period took forever. Other classmates must have been discouraged too because it was in Greenwad's sixth hour English, reading quietly about old Silas Marner that I had a firsthand visual experience with the birds and the bees. Danny Stodderback dropped a folded piece of paper on the floor, meant for Mike Schumaker who sat behind me. I got it with my shoe before Mike did and when I unfolded it, I encountered an anatomically correct drawing of a boy and girl whose private parts were touching. They were going all the way while standing up, Violet told me later when I asked her about it. Silas Marner was confusing and discouraging, but this was the worst. I was still pretty much in the dark about going all the way since health class sort of skirted around the issue with general details of reproduction, menstruation and ma-toor-a-ty without really putting anything together. Even when Cousin Boo had enlightened me in second grade when she said the dad had to roll over on top of the mom, it had been too horrifying to contemplate at the time. I mean I'd heard of doing it before but had never actually seen any actual pictures about it. Violet said I was a stupid jerk and that Danny Stodderback got a kangaroo court over it. The whole thing made me nervous. My imagination, being the way it was, went kind of haywire, trying to sort out the guy parts and the girl parts and kangaroos? I was worried. There was no way Silas Marner was getting much attention after this.

There was also no way to clear things up with Mom. The closest Violet and I ever got to a birds and bees talk with her was when she left Violet and me a couple of pamphlets about menstruation on our thirteenth birthday. No talking about it. No question and answer period. Just read it. Over and out. When Violet and I finally got our periods at fourteen years old, and it turned out we weren't himoradikes, which meant we were girls on the outside and boys on the inside, according to *The National Enquirer* and Violet, it was a trial of errors trying to figure out how to wear my sanitary belt and Kotex napkins. Most of the time, the whole contraption slid up my back.

Violet and I liked to go swimming, which might have been a talent. We'd been going to Lake Erie's Sterling State Park with Mom and Aunt Sophie and Boo since we were little. Sometimes Dad went and Hyacinth and Bobby. We roasted hot dogs on the grill and burned up marshmallows. Most of the time, dead fish floated on the water or laid on the beach with flies eating out their eyeballs. We steered clear of the open manhole designed to suck unsuspecting swimmers into its bottomless pit to the center of the Earth, according to Violet who heard it from Carol Jenkins who lived at the lake in the summer in a big white house behind a cracked Medieval structure call the breakwall.

Dad taught us how to dog paddle before we ever had lessons at the Y.M.C.A. One of my favorite pictures was of Mom, Violet, Boo and me sitting on a fallen tree at the beach. Aunt Sophie must have taken the picture because she's not in it. Another picture was of me walking past him sleeping on a blanket on the sand. I was five years old and looking puny with my bathing suit stretched out across my front. My dad was big and looking handsome, asleep in his t-shirt and jeans.

I had no other aptitude for athletics besides swimming and proved it by breaking my finger while catching a softball in gym class in sixth grade. After I fainted, Mr. Burns told me to hold my hand under the cold water faucet in the girls' bathroom. No one called Mom to bring me home and have Dad make me fried bologna sandwiches and put me to sleep in their bedroom with the curtains drawn. I guess it wasn't serious, except if you looked at my hand, one of my fingers was crooked.

I loved to watch TV, which I considered a talent. I knew what shows were on at what time and on what day. After school, there was *The Mickey Mouse Club* with Cubby, Karen, Annette and the rest of those guys. Later it was *Spin and Marty* on the cowboy ranch. When I was really little, there was *Howdy Doody*, *Kukla*, and *Fran and Ollie*, which I used to think was one whole word until Violet clued me in. Soupy Sales ate lunch with me on school days. I remember George Burns and Gracie Allen who had a magic television set in George's upstairs apartment so he could watch everything that was going on downstairs. When he said stuff to Gracie about things she did when he wasn't around, she got even more confused than usual. I remember Bob Cummings and his droopy dog Cleo getting into trouble with his housekeeper. When I was really little, Violet and I watched Cosmo Topper and his invisible friends who died in an automobile accident but came back to play tricks on him, making him look stupid in front of other people including his mixed up wife who got even more mixed up when he talked to her and them at the same time. Lawrence Welk and his Champagne Orchestra were a drag with the talented tap dancing Jimmy, but the Lennon sisters were cool, especially Janet. I tried to wear my hair in a ponytail like hers before Mom took Violet and me to the beauty shop for our summer pixie buzz cut hairdos. When the Beatles gave their first TV appearance in America, it was on *The Ed Sullivan Variety Show*. I thought I would die when they sang "I Wanna Hold Your Hand" in the TV room with Aunt Amelia, Mom, Dad, and Hyacinth talking the whole time. Mom said John Lennon looked like he had poop in his pants. She said the drummer looked like a bloodhound.

Everybody except Violet and me laughed. We sat up close, looking casual. I fought back tears over Ringo and told him so in a letter care of *The Ed Sullivan Variety Show*, which I never sent. I wrote it locked up in the bathroom. Sid Caesar and Imogene Coca were silly. I didn't like Red Skelton. Dad did, and Mom didn't. She hated clowns, and Mr. Skelton dressed up as one and cried every single show. Milton Berle rounded out the weekend slots along with Jack Benny and Rochester. *Wagontrain* and *Gunsmoke* were high on my list of priorities since Dad liked them, too. Hyacinth Suzanne was in love with Rowdy Yates on *Rawhide,* and it was one of the few times she and Mom and Violet didn't snap and crack their gum. I liked watching TV with just me and Dad the best because he didn't chew gum and he didn't talk, usually.

Probably my best talent was my imagination. Mom said was fertile, which was confusing since I thought fertile stuff had to do with guy and girl parts. One time, I walked home from piano lessons in the rain, pretending I was in the French Foreign Legion and dying of thirst in the desert. I did a lot of falling down and dragging myself across the Boys' Catholic Central High School practice field across from our house on Godfrey Street before we moved and neglected to tell Hyacinth. Piano practice had gone well, and I was feeling rather good about things. Clouds had gathered overhead before my lesson and by the time I got out, drops began to fall. Big round giant plops like small water balloons. I tucked my piano book in the waistband of the back of my shorts and dropped down to the ground, prepared for an enemy attack on all sides. My plane had been shot down, and I was lost on foreign soil. I had to keep my wits about me. No getting scared and acting like a girl. I'd been specifically trained for just this kind of situation, earning high scores for my unit. Through special night goggles worn only by the French Foreign Legionnaires, I scanned the horizon for the enemy, for any signs of life. What was that? I was sure something moved. There it goes again! I crawled on my belly, keeping my rear-end as low to the ground as possible. I checked to see if my valuable papers were still tucked away under my bulletproof vest. Yup, they were still there. I wiped sweat from my eyes with my forearm like they did in the movies. I blinked several times. I knew I'd finished the last of the water from my canteen hours ago. *Would I live or would I die? Would anyone know my plane had gone down miles into the red zone? Were my comrades looking for me now?* I knew I couldn't send a radio signal even if I had a radio because of the enemy being so close as they were, holed up in bunkers just the other side of those bushes. *Don't panic,* I told myself. *Think!* I reconnoitered my racing thoughts. I waited. I planned. It was now or never. I stood up, and holding my rifle in front of me, I made a dash for the nearest tree and almost kissed it in relief of getting there safe. One more obstacle to get through before making it out of enemy country and into the green zone where I knew other French Foreign Legionnaires were posted. After looking both ways, I marshaled my reserves and made a run for it, breaking through dense rows of wild thorny brush out of danger and into safety. I checked the folded papers under my vest and found them unharmed. I smiled to myself, thinking I'd probably earned a medal for my bravery and cunning.

"Lilly, are you alright?" Mom asked me from the shelter of the front porch steps. Violet stood next to her.

"Yeah, sure," I answered as I casually crossed the street after passing easily through the small hedge that marked the edge of the Boys' Catholic Central High School practice field.

"You're soaked," Mom said, as she watched me climb the steps. "What were you doing out there on the field? Your sister and I thought you might be hurt?"

She looked me over.

"You're all muddy! You should have taken an umbrella! Get your wet things off before you catch cold," she said as she walked into the house. "Violet, get your sister a towel."

"What a dope," Violet said, following Mom into the house. "You were out there pretending something, weren't you? Honest to Christ, Lilly, you are *muy weirdo.*"

Chapter 12.

SWEETDREAMBABA

I knew I was dreaming, and I did it anyway. My grandmother, as a young girl, sat on a rock, dangling her legs in the water like a mermaid. Small circles ringed out from her in the pond. I knew she knew I was watching her though she continued her quiet play in the water. I stood, looking at her across the pond, remembering our dream flight on the giant bird when I met her some time ago in my sleep when we all stayed over at her house, getting it ready to sell it. I stood, and she sat, knowing I was looking and she was thinking, but neither one of us did anything about it. The sun shone warm against my skin, washing me clean and whole. After a while, she spoke without looking up.

"I'm glad you came," she said, in her native Serbo-Croatian tongue which I understood without any problem.

"I miss you Baba," I said, easily in Serbo-Croatian as tears filled my eyes.

"I know," she said, looking up and seeing me on the far side of the pond. "Come and sit with me. Here." She patted the smooth silver-gray rock where she lounged.

Without thinking, I stepped out onto the deep aquamarine water and began walking across its surface to her. She wore a white lace apron. Her blond hair lay unbraided over her chest. She smiled as she watched me cross the pond toward her.

"The water is nice, yes?" she said.

"Yes," I said, looking at her. "It feels like Jello." I smiled and looked down at my feet atop the clear deep blue-green substance. "I thought it would be hard like glass, but it's sort of a semi-solid like Jello."

When I started considering the water's magic, I began to sink.

"Do not think, child," Baba said when she saw my ankles melting into the deep blue expanse. "Feel," she said. "Use your heart." She placed one hand over her own, and then touched her brow. "Not your head."

When I covered my own heart with my hand, I felt I wore an apron like hers but with a bib over the top and smiled as I passed my hand over my chest. I crossed the small lake, one foot in front of the other, my arms out at my sides like a tightrope walker, Baba keeping watch over me the whole time.

I walked slowly and easily toward my grandmother. We were two girls meeting again in dreamtime. When I reached the rock where she was perched, she extended her hand to me and guided me up to where she sat. Her silver-gray rock was warm from the sun and soft as a small animal's underside.

"Feels like a kitten," I said, drawing my palm over its surface. "I thought it would feel different. Hard."

"Things are not what they seem. You need to forget what you think you know about rocks and water and Jello." She smiled. "Yourself."

"I missed you Baba," I said, again meaning it with my whole heart. Drops spilled from my eyes, turning into diamond crystals where they fell upon the silver-gray fur.

"It has been difficult for you sometime, Lilly June. I know. I see," the girl Baba said.

She touched my hand, infusing warm strength from her fingertips into mine, easing hope and joy into my veins like spirit food. Answers to questions I never asked pressed into my heart. Like a silent movie, scenes from my life reeled by--sometimes fast, sometimes slow, sometimes like hours in detail. I saw my dad curl a strand of baby fine hair behind my ear while fishing on upturned pails at the lake. I saw Grandpa Jeda push me in an oversized baby carriage across the lawn of his backyard. I saw myself enjoy fried bologna sandwiches under the covers of my parents' darkened bedroom. I saw myself in Dad's arms, rocking with him in the big chair, a cool towel wrapped around my arm. I saw Mom dance and shout at a Serbian picnic with the Tambouritzans. I saw Hyacinth

Suzanne with her hand on my knee in our car under the streetlights. I saw Cousin Boo and I as friends everywhere. And my old Baba, my broken arm in hers as she filled it with good health. I saw only good and happy times. I saw the cloves and cinnamon gypsy with her silver and gold bangles nod to me, speaking through her eyes to me. She impressed in my mind the same word that the great winged bird had said to me before in my dreamtime. Suddenly, a long shadow spread overhead. The girl Baba and I looked up to see the grand eagle signal to us. It was time.

"I'm coming for you," he said, clearly in eagle talk. "Are you ready?"

Together, Baba and I rose upon her bunny soft rock. We held hands. The giant phoenix swooped down and hovered next us noiselessly. Patiently. He stretched out his dusty butterfly wing as a walkway for us to climb aboard his horse-widened back. I rode directly behind his neck. Baba rode behind me. Holding onto ourselves and our feathered chariot, we rocketed into the sky blue heaven. Up and up, faster and faster, we climbed into the luminous fantastic purple void. All sound muted in the opaque black light. I've been here before, I thought. I know this place. I opened my mouth to eat the joyous air. The three of us glowed brighter as our speed increased. Unafraid, we speared upward, bending into the wind like jockeys; the faster we flew, the more luminous we got. In our speed, we mixed and dissolved, stirring ourselves into each other and the glorious void. We shot out through the frontier. Expanding. Rushing and standing still. We burst into morning stars. Baba, eagle and I, the same vast one thing. No boundaries. No limits. No me. But all me. No Baba but all Baba. Me and Baba and the eagle all the same. All one. We were nothing and everything.

Laughter dispelled the experience. As if in reaching the apex of our flight, we hovered in time and space exalted. Shining ever brighter, we breathed in stardust. Molecules separated and coagulated, turning me into just me and Baba into just Baba and the grand giant phoenix into himself. We waited, anticipating the ride into the crest of our descent. And as if thinking made it so, we began our lightning descent. Baba leaning into me and me leaning into the neck of the bird. We charged into the fall, shooting through the void from black, to ink, to royal, to sky blue. In a blink, we braced over Baba's soft perch. Quiet sounds of the pond returned. A low, full melody of stringed instruments sang sweetly. The grand phoenix hovered patiently, again stretching his huge dusty wing for the girl Baba and me to a light.

Filled and empty at the same time, overjoyed and heartbroken, I became aware that I had all the answers to all the questions I'd ever asked or would want to ask, and none of it mattered. Moments in themselves were perfect and whole. All there was was now. All there'd ever been was just now.

"Did you like the ride on the back of my Googie?" Baba smiled.

"Googie?" I blinked. "Googie? This is Googie?! I thought he was a tin man who used to do bad things or Violet's bear. Well," I said, "until I found out it was Violet all the time. But this is Googie? *The* Googie?!"

"This is *my* Googie," Baba said, gradually speaking in heavily accented English, changing from the girl Baba of my sweet dreams into my familiar aged grandmother with wrapped braids and sensible nun's shoes.

"Your Googie?! I don't get it. I thought Googie was a pretend thing that my sister and I made up?"

"Yes. Googie is special magic. You've seen him before," Baba said, ignoring my questions.

"Yes," I said remembering him from dreams past, "but. . ."

"You can have him now. To keep you safe. Strong. I give him to you," Baba said. "He is yours. When you need him, you come to our place with water like Jello and rocks like rabbit fur. You call for him with your heart and he will come. He will take you for a ride to clean out your pains and make you full again. He will give you good food. Someday, when you are old, and you have a child who needs him, you bring her here and give her Googie. He was my Baba's Googie before me. He is mine, and he is yours. He is a gift to pass."

"Okay," I whispered.

"It is okay," she said, touching my hand and sending quiet strength through me. "It is okay to know things and to dream things. Sometimes there are more answers besides one. You find your own answers. You find your own Lilly. Stand now. You can stand by yourself," Baba said, letting go of my hand.

"Okay," I whispered, and stood up.

"Now you go back."

High overhead, circling like a winged cloud the grand bird, Baba's magical good Googie, and now mine, agreed. He spoke one single word into my heart in eagle talk.

"What?" I called up to him, shading my eyes against the sun.

He spoke again, but I could not hear him.

"What?!" I called out again. "Please?"

"Lilly! Wake up and go back to sleep. Dammit. Why do you leave your bedroom door open when you're going to holler in your sleep?" It was Violet. "At least you got a bedroom door to close," she said and pulled it shut. "Christ," she muttered as she shuffled away.

I lay on my back, arms crossed under my head, and thought about my dream. I wondered. And thought about my dream some more. And wondered again.

Chapter 13.

REALITY CHECK

I wanted to hug everybody the next day. I woke up feeling wise and perfect and full of love. I met Violet at the breakfast nook having a bowl of Raisin Bran. I ruffled her hair as I went by, and she backhanded me with her spoon.

"Hey!" she said, without looking up from her bowl. "Stupid."

"How is my twin sister this morning?" I asked, ignoring the spoon slap since I was feeling marvelous.

"How do you think I am?" she grumbled. "You kept me up all night, hollering in your sleep."

"I didn't know I was talking in my sleep. How unusual of me." I smiled for the sheer pleasure of it. "Sorry I woke you up."

I floated into the chair next to my feisty sister and poured cereal and milk into my bowl. I felt like I could do anything. Life was grand.

"Yeah, well next time keep your damn door shut," she said, shoveling cereal into her mouth.

"Oh," I sighed loudly. "I had a wonderful dream about Baba last night. Only she was young like us. It was wonderful, really. Maybe she was a couple of years older than us. She looked younger than Hyacinth but older than us," I mused in her memory, absently stirring milk and flakes in my bowl. "Anyway, she was a girl, not old like she was when she used to babysit us, and she was so pretty." I smiled. "She had this long blond hair that went down her back, and there was this huge eagle that we rode around on who could actually talk to us in eagle talk."

"What?" Violet slammed her fisted spoon on the table. "What are you yammering about?"

She looked at me sideways hunched over her bowl.

"A dream I had last night." I smiled sweetly.

"What's with that stupid grin on your face?" my sister said. "Makes you look retarded."

I looked at my twin knowingly. I was more mature now while she was so young and inexperienced in other worlds and magical Googies. What did I care what silly thing she called me? I was wise and full of love wrapped in the afterimage of my magical dream cocoon.

Violet slurped cereal milk from her bowl, stood up, shoved her chair back with her legs and left the table. I heard her clatter her bowl and spoon in the sink, walk out of the kitchen and stomp up the stairs to her bedroom.

Ah, well, so much for that, I thought. I closed my eyes, leaned back from the table, crossed my arms and conjured up my dream mates. Behind my eyes, I saw the beautiful girl Baba and me, cruising around the glittering black lit galaxy atop our large feathered friend, our Googie. We glowed. We radiated. We mixed and dispersed, then disappeared. We laughed out loud. We rode as happy voyagers, all the while emptying out the bad and filling up with the good.

I was still sitting in the breakfast nook daydreaming when Mom came in.

She said, "Lilly? What are you doing?"

She had a box of saltines in her hand.

"It's time you and your sister got going with your Saturday chores." She sighed loudly. "Whose turn is it to mop the kitchen floor?"

I showed her my face to her but not much registered.

"Lilly? Is it your turn?" she insisted. "And don't forget to wax this time. I've got a terrible headache this morning, and I'm not going to be able to watch you two every minute."

"Okay."

"Honestly," Mom said, turning from the doorway. She said something about me not being able to find my head with both hands.

I didn't mind my Saturday chores this time as the solitary work gave me time to hang out in my dream. I breezed through mopping and waxing the kitchen floor, washing windows, wiping down the table and chairs, and vacuuming the breakfast nook carpet underneath. I refilled the salt and pepper shakers for extra credit and added more paper napkins to the dispenser. I cleaned around the canisters on the kitchen counter top and scrubbed the double sinks with Comet. After that, I wiped down the front of the refrigerator and stove top. I swept crumbs out of the double oven. I filled a pail with warm, soapy water and went into the pink tiled bathroom behind the den. In the mirror, I saw myself and stopped. Something was different about my face. I leaned in. The golden halo between the pupil and blue-gray iris of my eyes was gone. Hmm. I wondered when that'd changed. I grinned big to check out my teeth as I hadn't had a chance to brush today, knowing good old Violet Jane would be sure to remind me. I breathed into my cupped hand.

"Yeesh," I said out loud. "Really better not forget."

"Standing in front of the mirror talking to yourself, again?"

Violet stood behind me.

"Do you and you have a lot to talk about?"

She opened the door to the linen closet, took out a dust rag and Pledge, and closed the door with her hip.

"Yeah," I said, feeling kind of giddy, "as a matter of fact we do."

"I saw in a psychology book at school that people who talk to themselves are mentally ill like Crazy Julia. Suppose you'll end up rolling your own cigarettes too," she said. "Christ, nothing around here is normal."

"Whatever you say," I said, smiling at myself in the mirror.

"*The National Enquirer* said there are people walking around the streets of New York and Chicago who swear at people walking by. Some of them are invisible."

"Who's invisible? The people talking to themselves or the talking-to-themselves people they're swearing at?" I said and laughed at my reflection in the mirror.

"What?" Violet squinted. "The people who are talking to themselves and other real and invisible people."

"How do you know the invisible people aren't really there if you can't see them?" I asked, having fun.

"Because you can't see them, dumbhead!" Violet was working herself up.

"I couldn't see them anyway since I'm here in Custer, Michigan, and they're on the streets of New York and Chicago," I said. "Isn't that where the people who talk to themselves and other people are, whether or not anyone can see them?"

"What are you talking about?" Violet turned it up a notch. She flexed her fist.

Normally this would've been about the time I'd have taken off to parts unknown, but since I was trapped in the bathroom, the only choice I had was to snatch the door behind me and lock myself in until the coast was clear. Normally I wouldn't have played like this with my tricky sister, but I was feeling particularly swell today.

"Christ." She shook her head. "You must've blown a gasket."

"You can never tell," I said to the mirror.

"Maybe you're turning into one of those *muy loca muchachas* since I can't ever figure out what you're talking about." Violet did an about-face and left with her cleaning supplies in tow. From somewhere in the house she said, "oooh, oooh, oooh," like she was ghost.

"If you think so," I said, more to my reflection than to her.

I closed the door and began the Saturday ritual of cleaning the bathroom. I even started singing about working on the railroad all the livelong day and couldn't I hear the whistle blowing since I rose up so early in the morn. *Dinah won't you blow. Dinah won't you blow. Dinah won't you blow your hor-or-ornnn!*

Time seemed irrelevant as I enjoyed my good feeling cocoon. I worked at my Saturday chores in a semi-conscious state, finishing sometime in the afternoon. With water-wrinkled hands, I made myself a crunchy peanut butter and strawberry jelly sandwich on enriched Wonder bread. I stole a handful of shelled pecan halves Mom kept in a high kitchen cupboard in a shoebox. I poured myself a glass of homogenized whole milk from a frosty quart bottle and carried my lunch into the TV room. Overhead, I heard the whirring of the sewing machine in Violet's room. Could be either her or Mom since they both liked to sew. The side screen door slammed. Could be either Dad gearing up for an outside job or Violet on her way to Barb's house. Hyacinth was at practice. Peering out the window, I saw Dad walk into the garage with purpose. Realizing I might possibly have the place to myself, by myself, I hurriedly set my lunch on the end table and turned on the TV set for some fortunate and unbothered television viewing. Alone, the place to myself, I settled on a Saturday movie on Channel 9, CKLW's Bill Kennedy's Showtime movie, already in progress. Bill smoked through a couple of cigarettes while telling me it was one of his Showtime's all time favorites. I sat down in Dad's recliner by myself. Upstairs, the sewing machine continued its work. In the backyard, the lawnmower did the same. I got up to close the window against the outside sounds and turned up the volume on Bill. I popped a couple of pecan halves in my mouth and took a long swallow of ice cold milk. *Yes, this was the life,* I thought: *A little television, a little peanut butter and jelly (not jam) sandwich, the place to myself. Ah, yes.* I cozied into the big chair. *Yes. Yes. Ah, yes.*

Bang, bang! One of the bad guys got killed on Bill Kennedy's Showtime movie, but I didn't mind. Outside the closed window, Dad and the mower walked the perimeter of the yard so that each successive circuit munched up grass thrown out from the previous swath. I didn't need to see it to know it as this was the routine. Around and around he goes, where he stops nobody knows. Something reassuring about Saturday sounds. Like things were really okay in the world. Like it was okay to have a bomb shelter that was your basement if you had enough canned goods and drinking water---and we did. What's with the Russians anyway? Who are they? And why do they want to drop bombs on us? Would Custer, Michigan, be a target because of the Nuclear Power Facility on Lake Erie? And how can a war be cold? Or hot, for that matter? What part of the basement was the safest? Did radiation get through cracks and cement? The whole thing was sort of scary if I thought about it much, so I changed my mind. I went back to TV with Bill.

I took a bite of my sandwich, and the alcohol and yeasty smell reminded me of the time our class went to the Wonder Bread bakery in first grade where we saw big steel tubs and cake beaters mixing up flour and stuff to make dough. We all got a small loaf, still warm from the ovens, to take home with us. Outside it was raining. I remember tearing out the inside of my loaf and rolling the soft cottony wad in a ball and chewing it; just about everyone on the bus did it. Being able to do it was almost worth the guilt and finger wagging from Mom when we got home. Violet said something about leaving the crust for Mom and Dad since they were always talking about how good it was, what with building strong bones and all. She figured the folks would be happy to have so much crust without worrying about the fluffy gunk on the inside. Violet said Googie told her to do it, and I agreed.

"Lilly?" It was Mom breaking into my first grade memories. "Where's your sister?"

"I don't know," I said, looking at my plate out of the corner of my eye, glad the pecans were gone.

"Are you done with all your chores?" Mom sighed, holding a glass of water in her hand.

"Yeah," I answered. "I was just having lunch."

"You need to be outside on a day like today, instead of sitting in the house watching television," she said, like I knew she would. "You're eating awfully late." She rubbed her forehead. "You'll spoil your supper."

"I forgot about the time," I said, looking up at Mom who suddenly looked awful. "I'll still be hungry for supper," I said, thinking Mom sort of looked like Crazy Cousin Julia with big dark circles around her eyes, which was sort of scary. Then somebody else got shot to death on Channel 9 TV with Bill.

"Uncle Drugo brought over a bushel basket of green beans." Mom put her hand to the doorframe. "They're out on the back porch. Get a Tupperware tub out of the cupboard and clean them."

"All of them?" I asked.

"Yes, all of them. Don't argue with me," she insisted. "I'm not feeling well. We'll have some for supper, and I'll can the rest later."

She walked over to the TV set and turned it off.

Just once I'd like to sit in the house, by myself, on a Saturday afternoon and watch whatever I wanted without being told to go outside. Just once would be nice. When I grow up I'm going to sit in the house all day and watch movies. By myself. With no one cracking gum or talking. And no one coming into the room and walking over to the TV set and turning it off.

Violet showed up while l was out on the back porch cleaning green beans. She plopped down on a lounge chair and squinted into the day. I pushed the bushel of beans over to where she could get at it with my foot. I dragged the plastic tub and paper shopping bag between us.

"Mom asked me where you were," I said, snapping the end off a bean pod and throwing it in the paper bag.

"I'll bet," Violet said, picking up a green bean and half-heartedly breaking off the tip.

"I thought you were upstairs sewing until Mom came down and asked where you were," I said, reaching for a handful of beans. "Did you go over to Barb's house?"

Violet let out a sigh.

"Yeah, for a while. She was going to the Country Club. Bonnie went too. Thought I'd get out of this place, but nobody was around."

Violet looked at her bean pod like it was a foreign object, wiggled it around, and snapped it in half. She threw its parts in the bowl, sighed and slouched back in her chair. We both watched Dad work at the lawn for a while.

"Do you remember the last time we went fishing with Dad?" Violet asked and darted a bean stem into the garbage bag.

"Maybe when we were in kindergarten." I said. "Maybe first grade?"

I snapped a bean into three parts.

"Yeah, maybe first grade," Violet said, picking at something on her finger. "So how come we can't do anything fun with him anymore? Why did we stop having fun? Like going fishing? Hell, I liked fishing."

Dad looked up at us from his circuit in the lawn. I smiled and waved with a bean in my hand. Violet just looked back.

"Remember how many bullheads we caught at Carter's Bay?" I said, thinking about the last prehistoric giant I wrestled out of the water. How much fun we'd all had.

I snapped a couple of beans.

"Well, so how come we stopped going? What? Did we suddenly get too old to go fishing in second grade? Or do anything but paint and haul crap around?"

125

She plucked a bean from the bushel and whacked it on the arm of her chair.

"I don't know," I said, snapping and tossing. "Wasn't Dad picketing at Consolidated? Maybe he was working overtime by the time we got into second grade."

"Yeah, well, seems like he could have found some time for us instead of Mom making us do all this damn crappy house work. Barb doesn't do all this crap. Barb hardly does anything. Bonnie either. Hell, I don't think Carol ever even makes her own bed!"

"Carol's got a maid," I said.

"Yeah, well so do we. Me and you," Violet said, viciously snapping a bean in half. "Other kids our age don't have to work their asses off. Why can't we just hang around once in a while instead of doing something all the time?"

"Yeah, I was just thinking, wouldn't it be nice to just sit around all day and watch TV sometime without someone walking in and turning it off right in the middle of a movie I was watching, or telling me to go outside and clean a mountain of green beans."

Violet sighed and flopped her feet on the floor. I looked at Dad.

"Both our parents work," I said.

"Yeah, that's just an excuse."

"Most of our friends have more money than we do," I said. "Barb's dad owns his own business and Carol's dad does too, and Mary's dad's a doctor, and Bonnie's dad's a lawyer."

"Whatever." Violet whacked a green bean.

"They probably never went fishing with their dads," I said, looking out at my own, suddenly missing him. I picked up a handful of Uncle Drugo's green beans and put them in my lap.

"Well, we don't go fishing anymore either, do we?"

Violet squinted into the yard.

"It's okay," I said, starting to feel a little heavy in my heart.

"It's not okay," Violet insisted. "We should be doing things together as a family besides us working all the damn time! By ourselves! We're always by ourselves. We're always The Twins!"

My brain started to clog up.

Violet said "Crap," and fell silent.

After awhile I said, "We play scrabble sometimes with Mom."

"Yeah, and she usually wins because she makes up words we never heard of."

Violet had a point.

"We just went to the slava as a family. Even Hyacinth went," I said, working at a couple of beans. "And sometimes Mom goes to church with us."

"Most of the time she sends us. And Dad never goes unless there's a funeral or a wedding. Look. Stop defending everyone! Sometimes I don't think Mom or Dad even care about us."

I didn't say anything.

Violet and I sat together for a while, watching Dad and cleaning green beans without talking, my heart getting heavier by the bean. Dad worked at the lawn like it was his job. Around and around he goes where he stops nobody knows. I wondered if he missed our fishing trips, too. It wasn't just me and Violet who had chores, it was everybody in our house. Mom and Dad and Hyacinth too.

When Violet said, "Sometimes I wish I lived in another family," my throat got tight. Thoughts got mixed up in my mind like mud.

"Nobody cares what's going on around here except us getting our chores done. Hyacinth's lucky; she's got practice all the time. She gets to escape. I feel more at home at other people's houses than I do here. People pay attention to me at Barb's house. They appreciate me. They think I'm funny. Her mom hugs me. When was the last time you got a hug from Mom or Dad? Or anyone for that matter? When was the last time anyone said I love you? Hell, I never heard anyone say they loved me or you. And you're supposed to be the good twin. Ha! The good twin. What, because you got blond hair you're supposed to be pretty and good? What's that make me? Ugly because I got brown hair? How stupid is that?"

Violet took a breath.

"Nobody gets me here. I might as well be talking to the wall." Her voice got thin.

Baba used to hug us, I know. And Dad did when we were little. And Mom let us sit on her lap once in a while. I had to think about the I- love-you part. I don't remember anybody saying it out loud to anybody.

"Can't remember, can you?" Violet looked at me.

I felt my warm dreamtime cocoon sliding down the drain. I put the girl Baba in front of my brain. I imagined her holding onto me while riding on our good Googie. Was that a hug? Did it count if it was a dream? Did the words I love you have to be said out loud?

"Well?" Violet insisted, staring at me.

"Baba used to hug us," I said. "She used to listen to us. She cared about us."

"That's one. Of course, she'd dead and gone now," Violet said. "Crap."

"I miss Baba," I said, my heart weighing about a hundred pounds.

"Me too," Violet agreed.

We sat together not talking for a while, squinting out into the day, our mountain of green beans snapped and cleaned.

Violet had a point. I was about as lonely as it gets. If I didn't plant myself in front of the TV set, living the lives of the families behind the celluloid screen, I lived in my own head, in my own fantasies, barely registering as a citizen of planet Earth.

When I was a kid, I wanted to be a Mouseketeer worse than anything. I dreamed of being best friends with Annette Funicello and Cubby and Karen and Jimmie, even if Jimmie was a weird old guy. I wanted the mouse ears and t-shirt. I wanted to belong. I wanted to be part of a TV family like the ones I watched for a half hour at a time. What if Miss Kitty could've been my Mom? She was always dressed up and I never saw her do any chores or ask anyone else to do any. I wanted people to sit around together and laugh and talk and feel good about each other like they did on *Leave It to Beaver* or *The Ozzie and Harriet Show* or even *Love That Bob*. I wanted someone, anyone, looking at me and acting like I was there and that I counted and wasn't it wonderful that I was part of their family? I wanted Violet Jane to like me. I wanted my Baba back. I wanted the Dad I used to have when I was five. I wanted to be carried in his arms and sung to and danced with. I wanted the smell of Old Spice on my cheek and his scratchy whiskers. I wanted to know someone cared.

Anyone. Sometimes I couldn't stop watching TV for fear the awful loneliness would swallow me up and eat me alive. (Once, when I was little, I got punished for carving my name in Mom's secretary, and I couldn't watch TV for a whole week. I stood behind the closed door and watched it through a crack.) I filled up my scary loneliness with other people's pretend lives. Television lives.

As Violet and I grew up, I spent less time with her and her friends and more time alone in my head or in the company of my TV people. I don't know what I did or thought about for some of the years between five and fourteen. Real life was a blur. I logged my years through my favorite TV shows.

"I think people need to hear other people they care about tell them they love them," Violet said, bringing me out of my celluloid thoughts.

"I see it on TV," I said.

"You see everything on TV," Violet said.

"It's nice to see people who get along," I said.

"Well, getting along isn't as easy as it looks," Violet said.

"I try to get along with you," I said, feeling brave.

"Yeah, I know," Violet admitted, "I know I'm sometimes *no muy facile*. I don't mean to be…*imposible* …but sometimes I just can't stand it anymore. I just can't stand being a twin. Half of a whole. What is that? Sometimes I just want to be one person. It's always The Twins this and The Twins that. I never get to just be me anywhere, except when I'm at Barb's or Bonnie's, and you're not around."

I didn't say anything .

"I'm not always running away from you all the time. Sometimes I'm just not being the two-headed girl," Violet Jane said. "I can't watch TV all the time, all day like you do. I've got to be around people, real live people. I don't want to hang out in my brain, day-dreaming all the time. I want to do stuff, not think about it. I want to talk to people. I want them to talk to me. I want to be in a family that acts like a family. Not like ours where you have to be cleaning something all the time, crap like that. Nobody can ever just sit around and do nothing. Ever. I hate it. You think you're alive when you watch TV. I think I'm alive when I'm at other people's houses."

I opened my ears as wide as I could, realizing my sister was talking to me about real things, and not yelling or calling me stupid or kicking or swearing. I listened with my whole being, knowing she was talking from her heart, knowing she would never say these things again or admit to ever having said them. I sat still.

"How can how you're born be such a big deal? How can blond hair be better than brown? Who made that up? Why should it matter what color your hair is? Barb's hair is brown, and nobody says she ugly. All the kids in her family have brown hair, and they're all cute," Violet said.

"Nobody said you're ugly because you have brown hair," I said.

"Yeah, well, when Uncle What's-his-name said I must be the smart one, so what do you think he was getting at?" Violet asked.

Again, I didn't say anything.

"The smart one. Ha! That's a good one. You even get better grades than I do."

"We get about the same," I said.

"Not according to our report cards. Don't you remember the crap I got for getting a B in English? Mom acted like I killed someone."

"You do better in gym class," I said.

"Yes, I do," Violet said, sitting up a little straighter.

"I am better in gym. Sports. Not that Mom or Dad care since we're not boys who play football. I can't do anything about not being a boy or not being pretty but I sure can do something about being in good physical shape. I can already do more sit ups and squat thrusts than you," Violet said. "I can climb a rope."

I couldn't even get up to the first knot, I thought to myself, with help.

"I can play soft ball and run faster, and my waist is only twenty-one-and-a-half inches."

The Scarlet O'Hara thing, I thought, but didn't say anything. We did the same amount of sit-ups and squat-thrusts during gym class, but I didn't contradict as I was trying to stay in the mood of the moment.

"Athletics is good. Keeping in shape is good. Speaking another language is beneficial. What if a whole bunch of Mexicans start living in the United States and *los solomente hablo Espaniol?* I'll know how to talk to them and understand what they're saying. *Comprende?*"

I felt the mood shifting. I felt the old Violet scratching to get out. I said, "I always thought you knew everything that was going on, and I never knew anything. You're cool and got stuff figured out. Everybody likes you."

"I got my eyes open. I pay attention to what's going on around me. I listen to what people are saying. I got my ear to the ground."

"I always feel left out."

"You can't expect to feel like you're part of stuff if you're always talking to yourself or daydreaming all the time."

"I don't understand people like Barb or Bonnie or Carol," I said. "I don't know what they want."

"What do you mean you don't know what they want?"

"When they're talking they talk about stuff I don't care about," I said.

"Like what?" Violet asked.

"Like what are the best clothes to wear, or who said what to who?"

"It's what real girls talk about. It's what's going on," Violet said.

"Isn't there more to it?"

"Like what?"

"I don't know," I said. "Like what do you dream about, or what do you think about when you're alone, or what about magic?"

"No wonder you don't have any friends," Violet said. "Wait a minute, that wasn't nice. I didn't mean it to sound so bad. It's just that you're so strange sometimes. I don't get how your brain works. Sometimes you act like you're from another planet. Sometimes you act like you're forty. And sometimes you're downright scary, talking to yourself, dreaming about Baba as a kid and flying around on birds and crapshit. What is that? How come you don't dream about boys or something like regular people?"

"I dream about whatever comes into my head," I said.

"You know you can make yourself dream about anything you

131

want," Violet said. "In The *National Enquirer* there was this guy who made himself dream about jumping off a bridge and hitting the bottom, and he died."

"How did anybody know what he was dreaming about if he died?" I asked.

"I don't know. They figured it out."

"You talk about The *National Enquirer* a lot," I said. "It's not science."

"Some of it's got to be," Violet said. "Can't figure out why you don't read it since it's got stories about extraterrestrials and stuff in it."

"I don't like to read."

"How come?"

"Ever since first grade when everyone laughed at me when I was reading out loud and couldn't get the word right," I said.

"I remember that," Violet said. "It took you a bunch of tries to get it right."

"Sort of killed the reading thing for me after that."

"That was first grade? You can read good now, can't you?"

"Yeah, but I don't like to," I said.

"Well, if you read The *National Enquirer*, you would like it."

"Maybe."

"So what's with all the daydreaming?" Violet asked.

"Stuff just shows up in my head like TV. Blocks everything else out. If I'm in school and the teacher is really boring, like in Social Studies, I just can't keep my brain on the material no matter how hard I try," I said.

"Me, either," Violet said. "That's the time I start sending notes or talking to somebody."

"Gets you into trouble," I said.

"Better than sitting around listening to that crap," Violet said. "Do you and Boo talk about dreams and flying around?"

"We hardly ever see Boo anymore. The slava was the first time in a long time. We were busy dancing and running around, sneaking up on you and Bobby." I smiled. "Do you really like cigarettes?"

"I hate cigarettes. They taste like crapshit, they stink, and they make me cough, but *los muy frio.*"

"They'll stunt your growth," I said.

"That's coffee."

"Mom said she drank coffee ever since she was a kid, and she's tall," I said. "Smoking's bad for you, especially if you want to be the best athlete."

"Maybe."

We sat quietly for a while. A shadow that looked like a large bird passed over us. The yard was evenly mowed, reminding me of the golf course behind Baba's house.

I said, "I liked lying on the grass at the golf course, looking up at the clouds."

"What brought that up?" Violet asked.

"Looking at the back yard."

"Pretty," Violet said. "You know, Lilly, you're a nice person. You like to see the good in stuff. And if there's nothing good to see, you make it up. Must be nice."

I was all over the map with this conversation and right now, I was feeling all warm and friendly. I hoped I would remember what my sister had told me about herself and our family and me, and how she said it.

"I always wanted to be you," I said.

"Me? But I'm not the pretty blond one." She wore a crooked grin and I wanted to get up and hug and tell her I loved her, but I didn't.

"Maybe not," I said. "But you're the spunky one."

"Spunky, huh?"

"Yeah."

"I guess," Violet said. "Let's get these beans in the house before we get yelled at. How about I take the garbage bag out to the garage and you take the beans into the house. Good luck staying away from Mom."

Chapter 14.

BUSINESS AS USUAL, SORT OF

The conversation on the back porch with Violet left me shell shocked. She had short-circuited my brain with her niceness. I wiped my eyes with my shirt shoulder as I watched her bound down the steps, grocery bag in hand, and trot into the garage. I promised myself I'd keep this rare bit of communication safely strung onto my silver cord of golden pop beads where all my good stuff stayed so I could drag it out when I felt bad.

I put the Tupperware tub into Uncle Drugo's bushel basket and wrestled it down the steps, pushing it in front of me with my legs. I set it on the cement driveway that butted up to the side door, then held the screen door open with my hip and picked up the bushel basket with the beans inside the tub. I plodded up the steps, pushing the bushel of beans in front of me with no help from anyone. In the kitchen, I found Hyacinth working at supper.

"Where's Mom?" I asked, dropping the basket to the floor.

"Upstairs, lying down," she said. "She's got a migraine."

"What're you making?" I asked brushing the dust off my arms.

"Pork chops, German potato salad, applesauce and green beans," Hyacinth said. "Here, put some of those green beans in this bowl." she handed it to me and smiled. "Wash them in the sink first."

I liked it when my older sister did the cooking. She acted like she liked it and tried new stuff she learned in Home Ec. She didn't bang and clank around kitchen like she was in a race, she didn't use every pot and pan in the house, and she didn't holler at us if we got too close. We could hang out in the kitchen with her if we wanted to, not doing anything. She could talk about stuff and cook at the same time. She was talented that way.

"I thought you were at practice," I said, washing the beans in the sink.

"Two hours ago," she said.

"Geez, what time is it?" I wondered, handing her back the beans.

"Almost four-thirty."

"Wow, time went by fast," I said, wiping my hands on my shorts.

"Sometimes it does," she said. "What were you doing that was so engrossing?"

My sister Hyacinth had good language skills, too.

"Talking to Violet."

"Really?" Hyacinth asked, like she didn't believe me.

"Yeah," I said. "She was nice."

"Really?" she wondered into the pot of potatoes.

"She came out to help me while l was cleaning beans, and we started talking about stuff and she was nice."

"Hmm," she said, wiping her hands on her apron.

"She said she never feels like anybody cares about her in our family and that nobody ever hugs us anymore or says I love you and that she feels more at home in other people's houses like Barb's and Bonnie's. She said she doesn't hate me, but gets tired of being a two-headed girl. She said that I like to look at the good stuff in things."

"She said all that, huh?" Hyacinth asked.

"Yeah," I smiled.

"Are you sure you heard her right?"

"Yeah."

"Will wonders never cease," my older sister said into a billow of steam, holding the lid in one hand over the pan of pork chops on the stove.

We didn't say anything for a while. I leaned against the counter out of her way, watching her cook. She put the meal together like she was conducting an orchestra.

"Why are you still practicing since you're graduating?" I asked her.

"There's still the Fourth of July parade. And the County Fair. I've got to march in those. The band needs help with so many of us seniors leaving."

"Isn't it hot in those uniforms?" I asked.

"Yes. They give me a rash," Hyacinth said, scratching her neck. "And my hat keeps slipping down my forehead. I wonder how the uniforms at Central are going to be."

"Are you excited about going away to college?" I asked.

"Sometimes," she said, stirring the green beans.

"I think I would be. And I know Violet would be."

"You think going away to school would be a great experience, but it's also frightening."

"How?" I asked.

"It will be a new environment. There will be new people. Most of my friends are going away to other schools except Margie. Central is three hours away one-way, round trip would be six. It won't be easy to come home every weekend."

"Would you want to? Come home?"

"I'd like the choice, but I don't imagine Mother and Father will want to make the drive," Hyacinth said. "Father didn't want me to go to college in the first place."

"Why? He didn't?"

"He thinks we girls will get married right out of college and waste their money."

She opened a can of applesauce.

"Dad said that?" *My dad?*

"It's what he told Mother," Hyacinth said. "She said they've been arguing about it for awhile because Mother thinks every girl should have a career to fall back on, that we can do more with our lives than she did as a legal secretary or at the employment office. She said we are all smart enough to be lawyers or doctors or whatever else we want to be, that we shouldn't depend on a man to take care of us. She thinks we're all too academically intelligent to stay home and become housewives."

Hyacinth tapped a spoon on a bowl.

"They both want us out of the house at eighteen." She tapped again. "Father gave in when I earned a scholarship to Central through band."

"I didn't know Dad didn't want us to go to college or that Mom thought we could grow up to be doctors or lawyers. I didn't know you got a scholarship."

I didn't know what went on in my own house.

I said, "That's cool about the scholarship. You must be good."

"Good enough."

"You don't sound very excited about it," I said.

"Last time I went to band camp. we moved and no one bothered to let me know about it."

"I remember that," I said. "How come nobody told you?"

"I don't know," Hyacinth said, turning the dials off on the stove. "I walked to Aunt Amelia's in the dark, carrying my duffle bag. She drove me to our new house, the one we're in now."

My sister lifted the two lids on the stove and put them back.

"She told Mother and Father they were irresponsible, that they should be ashamed of themselves."

"She did?"

"It was nerve wracking," Hyacinth said. "I had a stomach ache for a week. I felt it was my fault."

"What's your fault?" Violet burst into the kitchen. "Where's Mom?"

"She's upstairs, lying down with a migraine," I said. "Hyacinth's making supper."

Violet walked over to the stove. She lifted up a lid and steam rose up. "Hmm, pork chops."

"And German potato salad and applesauce and green beans," I added.

Violet put the lid back on the pork chops.

So what's with Mom these days? And her migraines? She's putting on a couple of pounds, too. Starting to get fat around the middle." Violet patted her twenty-one-and-a-half-inch waist. "Maybe she should do some sit-ups."

Chapter 15.

SIT-UPS WON'T HELP

Mom continued to have migraines. She threw up every morning before she went to work and when she came home, she went straight to bed. If Dad was around, he made pancakes and French toast for supper; if he wasn't, Hyacinth made real food. While we did whatever we did downstairs on tiptoes, Mom laid upstairs on her bed, in the dark, with a washcloth on her forehead. When I offered to make her a fried bologna sandwich, she stumbled out of bed and threw up in the toilet. Once, when she made it downstairs to eat supper with the rest of us, Violet suggested she do some sit-ups, to which Mom and Dad both told her to shut up. Mom left the table in tears with Dad in tow. Hyacinth wondered if Mom had cancer, Violet wondered if Mom and Dad were getting a divorce, and I spent a lot of time with Baba on Mars.

In the meantime, there was a graduation party to plan for. We girls split up some of the duties. For starters, since I had the best penmanship, I addressed the invitations. From her bed, in the semi-darkness, with her eyes closed, Mom told me to get the names and addresses off her Christmas card list that was in her secretary, which I should know about since I'd carved my initials in it a few years back. When it was Hyacinth's turn with Mom, she sat on the edge of the bed and wrote down the menu Mom dictated. Food would be laid out as a buffet so people could pick what they wanted from a big table with hot plates. Hyacinth called Aunt Sophie about how to arrange the house and yard for the big event.

When Aunt Amelia called one morning, she said, "The poor dear. Is she still sick? It will probably only last another month."

"Did you want to talk to her?" I asked. "She's upstairs lying down. Dad's out in the garage."

139

"Oh, no, don't bother them. I thought I'd see if your mother was feeling any better today," she said. "Maybe I'll stop in for a minute later. Just tell them I called."

On the other end of the phone I just said okay and hung up, but wondered how Aunt Amelia could know Mom would be sick for only another month. How could a person plan how long she was going to be sick? I guess Mom and Dad were not getting a divorce because she was getting fat like Violet said, but this didn't rule out cancer or any other weird disease.

"It was Aunt Amelia," I said to Hyacinth, who was eating shredded wheat with Violet and me in the breakfast nook. "She said Mom's probably going to be sick for only another month. How can she know that?"

"She's only seen Dr. Erickson once that I'm aware of," said Hyacinth.

"Dr. Erickson's Mary's dad. He's an OBGYN doctor who gives pelvic examinations and fixes girl problems," Violet said, shoveling cereal into her mouth. "And...delivers babies."

Her mouth dropped open and some Cheerios fell out.

"She's not going to have a *baby* is she? She's forty gosh darn years old! She's way too *old* to have kids! She could be a grandmother already! Crap and crapshit, what will my friends say?" Violet shoveled in another mouthful. "This is awful."

"Calm down, Violet. We don't know that Mother's PG. You're jumping to conclusions," sane sister Hyacinth said. "Maybe Mother has a cyst on her ovary or something."

"A what?" I asked.

"Yeah, and what's PG mean?" Violet asked.

"PG is an abbreviation for pregnant," Hyacinth said.

"Why don't they just say pregnant?" asked Violet.

"Because they're trying to be discreet," Hyacinth said.

"Be what?" I asked.

"Discreet?"

"Yeah."

"Modesty," Hyacinth said. "Women want to hide their bodies

and protect themselves when they're pregnant. They cover themselves up."

"Like Lucy Ricardo on I Love Lucy," I said. "She got big as a whale and wore blouses that looked like tents."

"So if Mom's PG then that means they're still doing it," Violet said, her eyes wide. "That's sick. I don't think I can finish my Cheerios."

Hyacinth pushed her chair back, took her empty cereal bowl and glass, and got up from the table. From the kitchen sink, she said, "You don't know what's going on. Just settle down."

"Yeah, but that's perverted!" Violet called out ,holding her spoon in her fist. "They shouldn't be doing it anymore! They're too old for all that stuff. Aren't you supposed to stop it after thirty or something? Mom's forty for Christ's sake! She can't have kids at forty. They'll turn out retarded or with three eyeballs like in The *National Enquirer*. What if we have a retarded kid in the family? Who'll take care of it? I'm not taking care of a retarded kid. I already take care of Lilly!"

Dad showed up in the doorway of the breakfast nook. He told Violet to keep her voice down, and didn't we know Mom had a headache?

"Is Mom PG?" she blurted out.

"Where did you hear that?" he asked.

"Aunt Amelia called and said Mom was only going to be sick for another month," I said, "and went to see Mary's dad who does OBGYN examinations. That's a doctor who delivers babies. Is Mom going to have a baby?"

"Aunt Amelia told you all that?" Dad wanted to know.

"No," Violet said. "She just said Mom was only going to be sick for another month. Then I said about Mary's dad and Hyacinth said Mom might be PG."

"Hyacinth didn't say Mom was PG," I said. "You did."

"Well, whoever said it, is she? Is Mom PG?" Violet was practically whining. "Is Mom going to have a baby at forty years old?! It'll be retarded. Or have three eyeballs and two heads or something."

"Might as well tell you girls now as ever," Dad said, taking a breath and looking at something on his hands. "Your mother is going to have another little one for us."

I jerked up straight in my chair, and Violet said crap.

"Watch your language, youngster," Dad said. "Wouldn't you like a baby brother in the family?"

I made a stupid grin and raised my eyebrows. Violet put her head down on the table.

Dad said, "Your mother is going to need all the help she can get since she's feeling so poorly. I expect you two to pitch in and help around the house. Can't expect your older sister to do everything."

Last week, Violet told me I was nice, now she tells me I'm retarded, again, and then I find out Mom and Dad are still doing it, and then Dad tells me Mom's maybe going to give us a baby brother. It was too much. I started to get dots in my eyes. I put my head on the table next to Violet. After a while, I looked up and saw that Dad was gone. Violet too.

During the next couple of weeks, Mom made more appearances downstairs after work. She walked around in a pale green bathrobe and carried a box of saltine crackers under her arm. She sighed less and looked better. Sometimes I caught Dad looking at her, googoo-eyed. When Violet complained to Barb's mom, Phyllis, about Mom having a retarded kid, Phyllis told her that she was forty when she had Barb's little brother, Michael, and he wasn't retarded. I guess that made everything all right. Plus, an article showed up in The National Enquirer where a woman in Argentina had twins at fifty-five years old, and neither one of them was retarded since one of them was reading Shakespeare in Spanish at two years old, and the other one was playing the piano at three---neither one had three eyeballs. That pretty much cinched it for Violet Jane, who now thought Mom might be brewing a couple of child geniuses.

By the time Hyacinth's graduation party rolled around, Mom was feeling pretty good. And big. She bought some frilly pregnant lady blouses and wore her hair like Lucy used to. She got into a cooking frenzy, making all sorts of exotic dishes in weird food combinations. She had a thing for lemon and sugar mixed together that she put on everything. She called it sweet and sour. Sometimes it was okay, and sometimes it gave me a stomachache and made my jaw hurt. Hyacinth's graduation party menu got changed around a few times to make room for Mom's latest concoctions.

Eventually, everybody found out about Mom's pregnancy. Hyacinth's big party sort of got run over by the possible arrival of another male in the family to "offset the estrogen factor" as Dad liked to say after reading up on some stuff he found in the World Book Encyclopedia that Mom bought from a traveling salesman who was working his way through college. Violet went to Kline's Department Store by herself and bought material and a pattern for a little sailor suit that she spent hours working on, which turned out to be convenient since the sewing machine was in her room, until Mom told her to cut it out when she was running it past nine o'clock at night. I bought a little mint green baby hat and booties since Baba told me in a dream not to put all my chickens in the same basket, that green was a "neutral" color.

Pushing her glasses up the bridge of her nose, Baba said, "What will you family do if your new baby brother is a baby sister?"

She was Old Baba in her wrapped braids and sensible shoes. She worked at a tablecloth with her crochet hook. I sat on the floor by her feet.

"Hyacinth said the same thing," I said.

"You need to hope only that the child is strong and healthy," Baba said. "Not too pretty in the face or people will make too much of it, and she will forget who she is."

"Or her sister will hate her for it," I said.

"Maybe so," Baba said.

It was good to be with Baba again. We sat in her house by the window that looked out across the garden. Tomatoes hung red on the vine and muskmelon grew plump. Orange poppies stretched on their stems next to blue irises. The sun shone clear and bright.

"Do you remember my good Googie?" Baba asked me after a while.

Yes, I did. Beautiful, giant bird whose back we rode on across the world.

"Yes," I said.

"Do you remember how I told you he is yours and mine to keep?"

"Yes."

"Do you remember he is to keep you strong? Help you stand?"

"Yes."

143

"Have you seen him again?"

I thought about it. I hadn't dreamed about him since riding with Baba when she was a dreamgirl, but there was a shadow like a bird once when Violet and I were talking on the back porch cleaning green beans.

"I saw a shadow like a bird once when Violet and I were cleaning green beans from Uncle Drugo."

Baba smiled.

"Was that my good Googie?" I asked.

"What happened when you saw the shadow like a bird?" Baba asked.

"I don't know," I said, looking back to that day on the back porch. "Violet and I had a real nice conversation. She said a lot of nice things to me." I thought a second. "She even said I was nice."

"Ah, you see?"

"Did the good Googie make her say those nice things to me?"

"I don't think he can do that, child," Baba said. "But he can make the air around you good and clean. He can make it not so much poison."

"Wow," I said.

"Don't forget him. He is always around. He watches for you."

"Thank you for giving him to me," I said. "I am glad he is my friend."

"He is more than friend to you, Lilly. He is to protect. He gives you a clean heart. He is exorcizing the bad Googie. Do you know what I say when I say this?"

"I think so," I said. "But I don't understand the exercising part."

Baba laughed.

"It is not making the muscle in your arms or running fast. It is exorcising. He is keeping the bad spirit from getting inside. The good Googie washes you clean so the evil thing cannot grow where there is only good."

"You mean like when you stuck a knife in Uncle Sava's door?" I asked.

"That?" Baba said. "That was something else."

"Oh."

"You know the bad Googie was your sister who put the apples in the toilet to make the water run over?" Baba asked.

"Yes, but not until I got older," I said, feeling dumb for it.

"You do not need to feel bad. You believed it was something different."

"You know when your sister makes trouble, she says it is the Googie who makes the trouble," Baba told me more than asked me.

"Yes."

"When your sister is bad, she feels she cannot change that part of her to make it good?"

"Sometimes I think she wants to be good, but can't," I said. "Dad says her mouth gets her into a lot of trouble. Sometimes she says stuff that hurts."

"That is the part I am telling you. My Googie, your Googie will protect you from the part that hurts from her mouth. He will close your ears so that you cannot hear you sister's words when they sting you. But not all the time."

"Okay."

"And one more thing I need to say to you, by the mouth of the good Googie, the word he says to you when he talks to you is stand. Stand by yourself. You are stronger than you think, child. You do not need your sister to hold your hand and lead you. You can walk by yourself. You can stand."

"Okay," I said.

"Good, now you go to dream about something like other girls you age dream about," Baba said. "You make a nice dream about Stevie Martin, that skinny boy who keeps riding the green bike past the house."

I got up from the floor of my dream and bent down and hugged my Baba.

"I love you," I said.

"I love you, too, child," she said.

When I woke up the next day, I remembered a scandalous dream I'd had about Stevie Martin and me. I rode on the handlebars of his bicycle down a forest path and neither one of us had any clothes on.

Chapter 16.

IS YOU IS OR IS YOU AIN'T MY BABY?

During the summer between eighth and ninth grade, Mom got as big as a barn.

"What the hell's she growing in there?" Violet wanted to know. "*Mi madre es muy muy largo.* Maybe we should call The *National Enquirer*. Might be a record. They said the biggest baby ever born was twenty-five pounds, two ounces, and came out talking."

I think she was taking bets with her friends about how big our newest addition was going to be. I think Dad was taking bets too, but not about size. One day I saw him pick up a mitt and raggedy old baseball from a trunk in the basement. I didn't know he had a hope chest.

"Hi, Dad," I said.

He turned around. "Hey Jack, look at this!"

He put on the baseball mitt and slammed the ball into it a couple of times.

I felt sort of important right then as I hadn't heard him call me by my childhood name in a long time. I touched the worn leather mitt.

"Is this from when you were a kid?" I asked.

"Here, put it on."

I slid my hand into the smooth skin on the inside of the glove and turned my hand over and over, looking at the laced top and darkened underside.

"Go stand over there, and I'll throw you a couple," Dad said, standing up.

"Inside?" I asked.

"Only a couple of throws." He smiled, and tossed me the ball.

I stuck out the mitt in front of me like I was warding off a tiger. The ball thunked against it and bounced onto the tiled floor, finally rolling under the wet bar. I scurried to find it, brushing off cobwebs when I did. I walked it back to Dad.

"You've got to let the ball come to you, Jack."

He lowered his own hand and turned it palm up.

"Hold your hand loose." He wiggled his arm. "Don't be afraid of the ball, can't hurt you with the mitt on."

I already had one broken knuckle from gym class and wasn't keen on earning another. I wiggled my arm and stretched my neck like they did on TV sports. I stood with my legs apart and hung the mitt between them. Dad tossed me another ball. This time I caught it in the glove, but it popped out onto the floor and bounced around before rolling under Mom's mangler. I got down on my hands and knees, retrieved it, and then walked over and handed Dad the ball.

"That's okay, Jack, you're doing better. This time, close your other hand around the ball when you catch it. Sort of scoop with the mitt and cover with your other hand," Dad said. "Show me."

I wiggled my arm and did a couple of shoulder go-rounds. In pantomime, I pretended to scoop the ball with my left hand and cover it with my right, trapping the ball in my mitt.

"Ready?" Dad asked.

He took a step back and lobbed the ball to me. I scooped it with my left hand and covered it with my bare right hand, just like I knew what I was doing all along.

"Heeeyyyy," Dad said.

"Pete, are you throwing balls in the house?" Mom called down the steps from the kitchen.

Dad made his eyes big like he was scared and put his pointer finger to his mouth.

"Just looking for something, Yoursies."

147

"I need you to look in the cabinet under the kitchen counter and see if you can find another bag of sugar. You know I have a hard time bending down," Mom said. "Who's down there with you? One of the twins?"

Dad nodded.

"Just Jack," I said.

"Jack?"

"Lilly June, Mom."

"What are you two up to? I hope you're not getting into anything you shouldn't?" she said. "Pete?"

"Yes?"

"I need you to help me," she insisted, from the top of the stairs. "But before you come up, check to see if there's another bottle of reconstituted lemon juice in the back room. I'm running out. If you can't find any reconstituted lemon juice, see if there's any apple cider vinegar."

Dad and I puckered our lips.

"Coming," he said, winking at me.

I heard her shuffle across the kitchen floor. I took off the baseball mitt and gave it and the ball to Dad who put them in the trunk. With a tiny ache in my chest, I watched him close the lid. Together, we walked into the bomb shelter to look for Mom's reconstituted lemon juice, knowing we had another one of her tangy experimental meals in front of us.

"What if Mom has another girl?" I asked Violet Jane while she worked at the baby sailor suit. The parents were out shopping and we were upstairs in Violet's combination room. She was hunched over the sewing machine fixing the buttonhole attachment to the presser foot---something I hardly ever did since the bobbin thread always seemed to gum up underneath my material, break off, and grind the machine to a halt.

"Crapshit!" Violet said. I guess she had problems with it, too.

"I wonder if everybody's going to be disappointed if it's not a boy," I said, slouched against the wall next to her bed.

"What's with this stupid, crappy machine!" Violet said, lifting the presser foot, opening the plate and taking out the bobbin. She pulled the thread out and started over again.

"I think Dad's got his heart set on a boy this time," I said, fiddling with a scrap of blue baby sailor suit material. "I think he used to treat us like his boys with fishing all the time when we were little, and painting the house, and our nicknames and all. I just hope everything's okay."

"Dad'll probably have a shit fit," Violet said, as the buttonholer did what it was supposed to do.

"You'd think with three of us girls the next one would be a boy. I mean, what are the chances?" I wondered.

"Remember what Mr. Brayburn said in math class? That if you threw up a nickel and let it drop, you might end up with fifty heads in a row, or fifty tails, or any combination."

Violet cut the thread in her teeth and started on another buttonhole.

I remembered what Brayburn had said, but couldn't get my mind around it.

"If it can happen with a coin toss," Violet said, "it can happen with kids. You only get two choices, boy or girl? Unless you get some weird thing like a hermadike, like I saw once in The *National Enquirer* where a kid's got a vagina and a dingis."

Violet sat up.

"Christ, I hope we don't get one of those. And I was worried about getting a retarded kid with three eyeballs!"

She went back to hunching over her project.

Violet and her *National Enquirer*.

"I just hope the new baby is healthy, whatever we get. I hope Dad's okay about it."

***

Central Michigan University opened its dormitories a week early for student arrivals, of which Hyacinth Suzanne was one. Mom had a hospital list, and this was on it. The doctor figured he calculated wrong and gave Mom only three more weeks until countdown, so my oldest sister was shipped off whether she liked it or not.

We got up at 6:00 a.m. as Dad wanted to get an early start. He drove three hours there and three hours back, stopping for gas once and only long enough to drag Hyacinth's suitcases into her dormitory room. Violet Jane and I went along for the ride, but not Mom, who felt crowded anywhere in the car due to her newly acquired largeness.

Before we left, Dad called Aunt Amelia to come over to babysit Mom while we were gone--- just in case. Violet made off with Aunt Amelia's latest edition of The *National Enquirer* and a box of chocolate covered doughnuts she'd brought over. Hyacinth sat up front, shotgun, not talking. Dad smoked a cigar and listened to the Tigers baseball game. I cracked a window in the back seat, making sure not to puke by reminding myself to not look straight down out the window at the asphalt as it raced by. Once in a while, Violet read out loud to me strange science from her newspaper. We both ate a doughnut. Or two.

Mom didn't look too hot when we got home from taking Hyacinth to college. She sat in a chair, rubbing her oversized belly. Aunt Amelia thought Mom'd eaten too much sweet and sour pork and had given her warm Vernors to settle her stomach. I saw Dad and his sister looking at each other like they knew something was up. Dad walked Aunt Amelia out the front door, and they talked awhile on the porch. He said something about this maybe being D-Day.

At about two o'clock in the morning, Dad knocked on the bedroom door, waking us up.

He said, "Your mother is on the way to the hospital."

I bolted upright. Violet stood up, eyes wide. Mom was already downstairs in the kitchen when we got there, holding her hand against the front of her skirt. Water was on the floor by her feet, and everyone's nerves got turned up a notch.

"I'm taking your mother to the hospital," Dad said again, picking up her suitcase. "Teresa," he said to Mom, "you wait here until I get the car ready."

"Hurry," Mom said.

"Holy crap," Violet said, forgetting where she was.

"Stop swearing," Mom said, remembering.

"Are you okay?" I asked Mom.

She didn't answer but made a scrunched up face like she slammed her finger in the car door and held her stomach.

"Crap," Violet said again, pacing, apparently unaware of her manners.

Mom didn't say anything as she started coming out of whatever had her belly tied up and shuffled to the top of the stairway.

"Wait for Dad," I hollered, taking her by the arm.

"Wait. Right," Mom whispered.

Dad bounded up the steps and got hold of both Mom's arms like he was helping a baby to walk. The lights were on inside the car and out of it. Together, Violet Jane and I watched Dad stuff Mom into the back seat and drive out of the driveway and into the street, but not before hitting the curb, making the headlights rocket up and down.

Great balls of fire and shit and shine-o-la," said Violet. "Great Googa Mooga."

Now what? I wondered, standing in a blaze of electric light, as someone had turned on every single lamp in the house.

"Should we call Aunt Amelia?" I asked.

"Hell, no," Violet said. "We're going into ninth grade. We're almost fifteen on our next birthday. We don't need no babysitters."

"I guess," I said.

"Can't get back to sleep now," Violet said, ready for a party. "Let's see what's on TV. Maybe shock theater or something creepy. But first, I'm getting something to eat."

In the kitchen, we raided Mom's stash. We made sundaes with Hershey's chocolate syrup and shelled pecans and melted caramels we put in a pan on high. We turned on an episode of Shock Theater that was on TV for some unknown reason and settled in for our treats, Violet in Dad's recliner and me sprawled on the daybed. We enjoyed ourselves in this way until Aunt Amelia showed up and crashed the party. She told us to turn out the lights and go back to bed. We took out sundaes to bed and kept the bedroom doors open, and Violet and I talked back and forth until our ice milk treats settled down.

In the morning, Dad came home and announced that we had a new baby sister. He said she weighed eleven pounds and eight ounces and was twenty-four inches long. He said she had a head full of black hair. He said she grabbed his finger right away when she saw him, and that our mother was doing fine. Dad said our mother had picked out a name for our new little sister. He said she was calling her Poppy Dee.

"Poppy Dee!" Violet said. "Another flower? What the hell kind of name is that?"

THE END

CPSIA information can be obtained
at www.ICGtesting.com
Printed in the USA
LVHW081456240321
682328LV00022B/164